Break a Leg, Liza!

Liza, Chris and Sam were watching a movie being shot on location near one of the Palm Pavilion's pools, when Liza suddenly gasped. The star, Miles Lockhart, was walking right toward her. "Ohmigosh, ohmigosh!" she sputtered nervously. "Here he comes."

Impulsively, Liza stepped forward so that the actor couldn't miss her. She was dying to meet him, hoping this was her big break. She gazed up at him and their eyes met. "Excuse me, miss," he said. "Is there some place where we can get beach towels?"

"Wow!" cried Liza. "How did you know I work here?"

Miles Lockhart smiled. "You *are* wearing the hotel uniform, aren't you?"

Liza looked down at her white polo shirt with the hotel crest on it and giggled nervously. "I guess I am. That's a dead giveaway, isn't it?"

"Yes," he agreed. The star stood there a moment, looking at her expectantly.

"Oh, the towels, yes. Come right this way; I'll get them for you," said Liza. She turned sharply and stepped . . . right into the *pool*.

**Look for these other books in the
SITTING PRETTY series:**

SITTING PRETTY
LIZA'S LUCKY BREAK

by Suzanne Weyn

Troll Associates

For David Young—A good friend
and an astute but kindhearted critic

Library of Congress Cataloging-in-Publication Data

Weyn, Suzanne.
  Liza's lucky break / by Suzanne Weyn; cover illustration by Joel
Iskowitz.
    p.   cm.—(Sitting pretty; #3)
  Summary: Working as a babysitter at the exclusive Palm Pavilion
Hotel, Liza risks her job when she tries to get a part in a movie
being filmed at the hotel.
  ISBN 0-8167-2007-X (lib. bdg.)   ISBN 0-8167-2008-8 (pbk.)
  [1. Hotels, motels, etc.—Fiction.   2. Babysitters—Fiction.
3. Performing arts—Fiction.]   I. Title.   II. Series: Weyn,
Suzanne. Sitting pretty; #3.
PZ7.W539Li   1991
[Fic]—dc20   89-77117

A TROLL BOOK, published by Troll Associates,
Mahwah, NJ 07430

Copyright © 1991 by Troll Associates, Mahwah, New Jersey
Printed in the United States of America.

10   9   8   7   6   5   4   3   2   1

Chapter One

Liza Velez leaned back on one elbow. With her free hand, she shaded her eyes against the glare of the morning light. Peering down the creamy shoreline of Castaway Beach, she searched for the three boys she knew would soon appear. Beside her on the wide, frayed blue blanket, lay her two best friends, Sam O'Neill and Chris Brown, half asleep, soaking in the sun.

Lazily, she pulled the front strands of her hair forward and examined the red highlights she'd streaked into her own dark brown hair. The sunlight made them glisten with coppery tones.

It had been a struggle to convince her mother that, at fourteen, she wasn't too young to highlight her hair. Now she wasn't sure if she liked the effect or not. *I hope it doesn't look too phony*, she worried. In this town of sunny Florida blondes, she wanted something that would give her the same natural, sun-kissed look, but wouldn't clash with her olive skin and dark eyes.

Suddenly, three tall figures carrying surfboards emerged from the cluster of palm trees that separated the beach from the country road behind it. Liza brushed the sand off her bathing suit and sat up straight on the blanket. "There they are!" she said excitedly to her friends. "Act like you don't see them."

Chris propped herself onto her elbows. Shaking her chin-length, strawberry-blond hair, it seemed to take her a minute to realize what Liza was talking about. She rubbed the back of her hand across sleepy hazel eyes. "Don't see who?"

"Boys," Liza said impatiently. "That's why we're here."

"I thought the point of being here was to see them," said Chris, quickly putting on a large cotton shirt over her navy blue one-piece suit.

"No, we want them to see *us*," Liza corrected. "And don't cover yourself up, you look fine."

"I look fat," Chris protested. The extra ten pounds which Chris was always battling gave her a soft, slightly pudgy look. Being seen in a bathing suit was torture to her. "I wish I was an Eskimo," she grumbled. "Then I'd be covered in furs all the time and nobody would know how much I weigh."

"You guys are crazy," said Sam, still half asleep. "I don't know why I even let you drag me out of bed this morning."

Liza looked back at Sam. The tanning oil on Sam's lean, athletic body shone. With a red visor shading her face, yellow zinc oxide on her nose, and her new blue-green tank suit, Liza thought Sam looked like the tropical parrot fish that swam in the local waters around the town of Bonita Beach. "That suit looks cute on you," Liza said, turning back to look at the approaching boys.

"Thanks," Sam answered. She pulled off her visor and ran a hand through her long, sun-bleached hair. "But don't try to butter me up. I'm not getting up this early again." Sam checked her waterproof black plastic watch. "Those guys didn't show until eight-thirty and we've been here since seven."

"I didn't know how early they'd arrive," Liza defended herself. "We'll do the same for you when there's a boy you like. Boys don't always realize that they like you. Sometimes you have to be around them and give them a chance to see that they've liked you all along."

"Did that guy you met on the snorkeling trip ever call you?" Chris asked Sam.

"No, and I don't care if he does," Sam answered as she rolled over onto her stomach. Sam was, in fact, disappointed that the boy hadn't called, but she often hid her true feelings by acting gruff.

The boys were now only several yards away. Liza's eyes were locked on Eddie Moore. He was tall and tanned with wavy, dark hair and slightly muscular arms. Liza couldn't see his eyes at that distance, but she remembered that they were bright blue.

"They're heading right into the water," said Chris, alarmed. Her eyes were on Bruce Johnson, Eddie's blond companion. "They're not even going to see us."

Liza jumped to her feet. "Come on," she said to Chris, heading toward the boys.

"We can't just walk over there," Chris objected as she began buttoning up her shirt.

"Sure we can," said Liza. "And leave that shirt open."

"I'll leave it open when I lose weight." Chris got to her feet and pulled at Sam's arm. "You have to come, too."

"Why?" Sam protested.

"You have to say hi to Lloyd. That'll make it seem more natural," Chris explained.

"Man," Sam groaned. "I see Lloyd all the time. I can't take him this early in the morning." Lloyd was the third boy in the group. He dated Sam's older sister, Greta. At nineteen, he was the surfer king of Bonita Beach. The surfers idolized him, but Sam could barely tolerate his empty-headed addiction to surfing.

Sam and Chris followed Liza down the shoreline. Bruce spotted them first and waved.

"He's waving!" Chris whispered happily, waving back.

"Of course he is," said Liza. "He knows us. We work with him, don't we?" Bruce worked as a pool boy at the Palm Pavilion Hotel, where the three girls were employed as staff baby sitters. Up until then, he'd simply been an older kid who didn't know Chris was alive, even though she was only two grades below him.

"No work today?" Bruce asked as the girls approached.

"Afternoon shift," Liza said. "We figured we'd make the most of it and hit the beach early."

"Good idea," said Eddie. "It's going to be a scorcher."

Liza and Chris had met Eddie at the beach one day when he was surfing with Bruce. Today they just

4

happened to be there because Liza had checked Bruce's work schedule to find out when he was off. She figured Eddie would be with him because the boys surfed at Castaway Beach every chance they got.

"You're lucky you don't work," Liza said to Eddie. "You can hang out all day."

"I do work," said Eddie. "I deliver for Flamingo Pizza, but today I don't start until four."

"I don't work," Lloyd volunteered proudly. "A job would seriously interfere with my surfing time."

"And what a tragedy that would be," muttered Sam.

"Absolutely," said Lloyd, not picking up on Sam's ironic tone. He flipped his white-blond hair out of his eyes, a gesture he repeated at least once every ten minutes. "To surf is to live."

"That's very profound, Lloyd," Sam said dryly.

"That's why I like Flamingo Pizza," said Eddie. "Nobody orders pizza before noon, so I can always surf in the mornings. And it's easy work."

"What a great job!" said Liza, keeping up the conversation.

"It's okay." Eddie shrugged.

"To drive around and not have a boss looking over your shoulder must be amazing," said Liza. "I would love it. That Mr. Parker, the manager at the Palm, practically drives me insane. He drives everyone crazy."

"Parker *is* a pain," Bruce laughed. "And you'd better stay out of his way this week."

"Why?" Chris asked.

"Because they're filming a TV movie at the hotel."

5

"They're what?" Liza shrieked. "Say that again."

"I said, they're filming—"

"I heard you," Liza cut him off. She staggered back dramatically, her hand over her heart. Liza's dearest, fondest dream was to be an actress. She'd always assumed that some day she'd be able to pack her bags and leave Florida to head for Hollywood, California. But now fate was doing her a favor. Hollywood was coming to her. "This is unbelievable," she gasped. "Who's going to be in the movie? No, don't tell me. If it's someone great, I won't be able to take it."

"Okay, I won't tell you," said Bruce.

"I can take it. Who?"

"Miles Lockhart and Luna Collins."

Liza closed her eyes. She wanted to scream with excitement, but Eddie was there and she didn't want him to think she was a lunatic. "That's going to be very exciting," she said calmly.

"You took it pretty well," Bruce teased.

"Oh, I know, but I'm just faking," Liza blurted out impulsively. "It's just so exciting."

"I think Miles Lockhart is goofy," said Eddie. "All that long wavy hair. Why doesn't he get a haircut? The guy must be forty."

"You're right," Liza agreed hastily. "He's not my favorite. I liked him when I was a kid and he was on that show about the family stuck on a desert island, *Treehouse on Little Island*. But he's much too corny for me now."

"You think Miles Lockhart was corny in *Treehouse on*

6

Little Island?" cried Lloyd, aghast. "I never miss the reruns. That show is totally great! I love the way those kids are always doing heartwarming stuff. That show really gets me."

"Those waves are breaking great," Bruce pointed out. "Let's get them while we can."

"See ya around," said Eddie. In another minute the boys headed out through the crashing surf, their boards under their arms.

"Tell Greta I'll call her later," shouted Lloyd.

"See you at work," Bruce called over his shoulder.

"You think Miles Lockhart is corny?" Chris asked, watching Bruce catch a wave.

"I just had to say that. I didn't want Eddie to think I was a twerp. I love Miles Lockhart. He's totally adorable."

They watched the boys ride the waves a little longer and then headed back toward their blanket. "I have to get into that movie," Liza said anxiously.

Chris shook her head ruefully. "I knew this was coming."

"Don't act like I'm crazy," said Liza. "This is a one-in-a-million chance. I mean, Hollywood is thousands of miles away. And I can't go until I'm at least eighteen. That's four years and thousands of miles between me and stardom. This could be my big break. If I get into this I could be a teen star—even have my own hotline number."

Liza held an imaginary phone to her ear. "Hi, this is Liza," she said in a high, perky voice. "I had bran flakes

7

for breakfast this morning. This afternoon I'm going to jog forty miles. I keep trim by eating right and exercising. Don't miss my exciting new movie, *Teen Dream*, co-starring Miles Lockhart."

"Do you really think people would pay a dollar a minute to hear that?" asked Sam, dusting sand from her feet as she stepped onto their blanket.

"Sure they would. They pay more than that for much dumber stuff," said Liza. Liza suddenly found herself daydreaming about a video in which she was the star. She was singing her number-one hit record. Then a commercial came on for the Liza Velez Hotline.

It was so vivid. *It's fate, destiny,* she told herself. Stardom awaited her. For Liza, the question was not *could* she do it. It was how? And when?

The video played on in her imagination. Liza shut her eyes and swayed with the music in her head. "Ooooooh, baby," she crooned, improvising the words and music. "Yeah, I got to dance." She shook her hips and danced on the corner of the blanket.

"What's gotten into you?" Sam asked.

"I'm just imagining my first video hit," Liza answered, still swaying to the beat in her head. "This is it. This is my big chance. Once I get into that movie there'll be no stopping me."

"Forget it, Liza," Sam warned. "You know Parker's rule about bugging the famous guests. It drives him bats. And he already thinks the three of us are flake cases."

"You just have to be more careful around him, Sam," said Liza.

"Me!" Sam exploded. "I only get into trouble because you guys always involve me in your nutball schemes."

Since they'd begun working at the Palm Pavilion over a month ago, Liza and Chris had managed to get into one mishap after another. Sam was always somehow swept along in the tide of their misadventures. . . .

Like the time Liza tried to sneak into a suite occupied by the rock group Cosmic Space Monsters—and she and Sam wound up face-to-face with an armed security guard. Or when Sam swam into the ocean to rescue two of Chris's young charges—only to have Mr. Parker blame Sam for not having been more careful!

Sam shook her head and sighed, remembering several such escapades. "Look, Liza," she said, "you'd better be cool about this."

"I'm always cool," replied Liza, a twinkle in her brown eyes.

"Yeah," Sam cracked, "but that doesn't mean you still can't get burned."

Chapter Two

Sam steered her bike up the horseshoe-shaped, white-gravel drive of the Palm Pavilion. She stopped beneath one of the palm trees that lined the drive, and waited for Liza and Chris to catch up. Being the most athletic of the threesome, she was inevitably in the lead when they biked to work each day.

No matter how many times she saw it, the grand hotel always impressed her. It was so unexpected, there on the outskirts of the slightly seedy town of Bonita Beach. Its many windows sparkled under crisp white canopies. Rose-colored walls gave the large building a cool, elegant presence as it stood regally in the center of lush grounds.

"Biking to work in the afternoon is dumb," griped Chris, pulling her bike alongside Sam. "Florida summers are too hot."

"I'll say," Liza agreed, joining them. "Now I'm all sweaty."

"Come on," Sam urged. "It's almost one. We'll be late." They headed up the bustling driveway where taxis, cars and tour vans picked up and dropped off the well-to-do guests. The girls chained their bikes to the bike rack and scooted between the daily delivery trucks and into the hotel's service entrance.

"I don't see any signs of a movie being filmed," commented Chris. But no sooner were the words out of her mouth than two huge silver trailers pulled into the driveway behind them.

"Even the movie trucks are awesome," Liza sighed. For a moment the three girls stood with their mouths slightly opened, watching the shiny vehicles make their way slowly, like silver dinosaurs, into the parking lot behind the hotel.

"We'll be late," Sam reminded them, pulling Liza and Chris through a screen door and into a small hallway. There they found their time cards and punched in. They went through the kitchen, then through the empty restaurant, and emerged into the elegant lobby of the Palm Pavilion. Mahagony columns spiraled up to the cathedral-type ceiling with its wide skylights, and lush palms thrived in brass pots.

The girls passed the curving front reception desk and went over to the bulletin board where each day's assignments were posted.

"Darn," said Chris, looking over the list. "Jannette Sansibar is back from vacation." Jannette was Chris's chief rival for Bruce's attentions.

Sam studied the list. She and Chris had house service,

which meant there were no children for them to baby-sit. Instead, they'd handle odd jobs around the hotel.

"Hey, Liza," Sam said, continuing to scan the list, "guess who you'll be playing checkers with this afternoon?" Sam waited for Liza to moan. Old Mr. Schwartz—whom Liza called the world's oldest living creature—had been vacationing at the Palm all summer. He often specially requested Liza as his checkers partner.

Chris saw the assignment and chuckled. But when there was no response, both girls turned. Liza was halfway across the lobby, heading for the plate-glass doors that led to one of the hotel's three pools—where the movie crew was setting up a scene.

Exchanging panicked expressions, Chris and Sam ran after Liza. "You can't go out there," said Chris, catching up with Liza first. "If Parker sees you, you're dead. Besides, Mr. Schwartz will be waiting."

"That guy is always late," said Liza, walking faster. "It takes him a hundred years just to walk down the hallway from his room."

"Please don't go out there," pleaded Sam, joining them. "Can't we just have a single week without one of us getting into trouble?"

Undaunted, Liza stepped out onto the pool deck with Sam and Chris close behind her. The pool closest to the hotel had been cleared for the movie crew. Powerful lights on tall metal poles were set up around the pool. A group of actors in bathing suits stood off to the side, looking bored. Standing at the shallow end of the pool was the actress Luna Collins dressed in a silver bathing

12

suit, her long blond hair cascading in curls down to her slim waist. And standing at the pool's edge, wearing a red cotton shirt and tan pants, was Miles Lockhart.

"I guess we can take a quick peek," Sam muttered, spotting the actor. She blinked at the sight of him. He didn't look quite right to her; she wasn't used to seeing him life-size and without a TV boxing in his image. He looked so much taller in person. She held her two hands up, made a square with her thumbs and forefingers, and framed him inside it. "Now he looks the way I'm used to seeing him," she said to Chris.

Chris nodded and Sam knew she was busy running through her mental file of trivia on the star. Chris's passion was TV trivia. She knew everything about anybody who'd ever been on TV.

"He's gorgeous, even if he is old," said Liza.

"He must be about thirty-eight," said Chris. "I remember reading that he was only twenty when he was in *King Corral* and that was exactly eighteen years ago."

"Aren't they showing that in reruns again?" asked Sam.

Chris nodded. "He was in *King Corral* for five years and then made a few movies, which no one ever remembers."

"Except for you, I'm sure," joked Liza.

"Naturally. They were *Swamp Teen*, *Motorcycle Vampires* and *Prehistoric Warrior*. His career seemed like it was almost over, but then he came back big with *Treehouse on Little Island* which ran for seven years. Now he directs and stars in his own series."

13

"Angelfire Road," Liza sighed. "I watch it every week. Did you see the one last week when—" Liza suddenly stopped short. Miles Lockhart was walking right toward her. "Ohmigosh, ohmigosh!" she sputtered nervously. "Here he comes!"

Impulsively, Liza stepped forward so that the actor couldn't miss her. She gazed up at him and their eyes met. "Excuse me, miss," he said. "Is there some place where we can get beach towels?"

"Wow!" cried Liza. "How did you know I work here?"

Miles Lockhart smiled, and his white, straight teeth seemed to glisten in the sun. "You *are* wearing the hotel uniform, aren't you?"

Liza looked down at the white polo shirt with the hotel crest that she wore over her own shorts and giggled nervously. "I guess I am. That would be a dead give-away, wouldn't it?"

"Yes," he agreed. The star looked at her expectantly.

"Oh, the towels. Come right this way, I'll get them for you," said Liza. She turned sharply and stepped . . . right into the pool.

Sam covered her eyes as Liza hit the water with a splash. A quick nudge from Chris made her open them again. "Look who's coming," Chris whispered urgently.

"Oh, shoot!" gasped Sam. Mr. Parker was walking in his usual officious manner toward the pool. He was wearing khaki Bermuda shorts belted high on his thin stomach, a short-sleeved, tailored shirt buttoned to all but the very top button, and sandals with socks.

"He saw Liza," said Sam. "She's dead. The three of us are fired for sure this time."

14

Mr. Parker stood across the pool from them and glared down at Liza. Liza swam toward the opposite end of the pool. She could feel Mr. Parker's eyes follow her. Mr. Parker continued to watch her and then caught sight of Chris and Sam.

Sam met his stare and smiled sheepishly. Soaked, Liza joined her friends. "I'm mortified," she muttered between clenched teeth.

"I think we'd better get out of here," said Chris.

It was too late. Mr. Parker had already made his way around the pool and was upon them. "All right, ladies," he said, his voice taking on the eerily calm tone he used when he was furious. "My hands are full today. I have a movie being filmed here. I have a convention of Plucky Chicken salespeople to prepare for. The air conditioning on the fourteenth floor is out. Chef Alleyne refuses to cook without his favorite wine, which the bartender forgot to order. And Mr. Schwartz is—even as we speak—banging his cane on the lobby floor demanding to know where his checkers partner has gone."

"Gee, I was just on my way in to—" Liza began to explain.

Mr. Parker held up his hand for silence. "Don't. Don't even try to explain. By now, Miss Velez, the sight of you floating fully clothed in the middle of the pool during the filming of a TV movie should come as no surprise to me."

"You see, Mr. Lockhart asked me for—" Liza tried again.

"Don't try my patience with excuses, Miss Velez," Mr. Parker spoke angrily. "This is the last—"

15

"Are you all right?" Miles Lockhart asked as he walked toward them.

"Allow me to apologize," said Mr. Parker. "I assure you—"

Once again Miles Lockhart flashed his perfect Hollywood smile. "There's no harm done," he said. "But I do need those towels."

"Yes, sir, right away," Liza spoke up.

"*You* will play checkers with Mr. Schwartz," Mr. Parker told her. "I will bring the towels personally."

"Thanks," said Miles Lockhart. Still smiling, he turned back to his actors and crew and called for a five minute break.

Mr. Parker's focus shifted to Chris and Sam. "And what are you two, her bodyguards? The three of you, get inside and work!"

The girls walked briskly to the hotel and didn't stop until they reached the back door. "That was a close one," said Chris.

"I'll say," Sam agreed.

Liza wrung her hair out onto the wooden floorboards of the deck. "This is so humiliating," she moaned. "How will I ever get into this movie now?"

Chris grinned. "I just remembered something. Miles Lockhart got his big break when he accidentally slipped on a banana peel in front of the director. He was a deli delivery boy, bringing in lunch. I read that in *One Hundred Trivia Facts*."

"Yeah, so?" asked Sam.

"So maybe Liza's fall will remind him of his own start, and he'll like her for it."

"He *was* extremely nice about it," Liza said, brightening. "Maybe that was lucky, after all. He's sure to remember me as a klutz. It might endear me to him."

"Somebody better endear you to Mr. Schwartz," Sam said.

"All right," said Liza. "Do me a favor. Go in and tell him I'll be right there."

"Liza!" cried Sam. "You have to come in *now*."

"I'm coming. I just want to go over and talk to those actors and find out how they got into the movie and if they need extras."

"Parker will kill you if he sees that you're still here," said Chris.

"I'll be quick," Liza promised.

"You're asking for trouble," warned Sam, turning to go into the hotel.

"Maybe, but I just have to get into this movie," said Liza. "I *have* to. And that grouch Parker isn't going to stop me!"

Chapter Three

"You were so lucky that you didn't get caught today," Chris said to Liza as they biked home that evening. They had already left Sam off at her house, and were heading down Vine Street.

Liza smiled. "I *was* lucky, wasn't I? And now I know exactly what I have to do to get into the movie."

"I can't believe you ran into a production assistant. How did you know that's what she was?" asked Chris.

"I didn't know," said Liza. "I thought she was an actress, so naturally I figured she'd know how to get into the movie."

"And that's when she told you about the videotape thing?" Chris asked as they slowed to a stop at a red light.

Liza nodded. "Yep. She said every actor on the set had sent in an audition tape. Luna Collins was the only exception." Liza had then gotten up the nerve to ask if there were any openings for extras on the movie. The woman acted cold at first, but suddenly smiled and told her that Miles Lockhart had decided he needed a new ending for the movie, one that would require more extras!

"I mean, is it luck or is it *luck*?" asked Liza as the light turned green and they began to ride again. "I asked if they need extras, and it just so happens that they do. See what I mean? It was meant to be!"

The girls stopped at the corner of Vine Street where they would go their separate ways. "Now don't forget," Liza said. "I'm counting on you to bring over your father's video camera tomorrow. If he says no, call me tonight so I can try to find another. I want to give Miles Lockhart my audition video as soon as possible."

"Relax," said Chris. "My father lets me use his camera whenever I like."

"Okay, see you tomorrow," said Liza, riding up Hibiscus Road. She pulled her bike into the driveway of a small, white stucco house with a red door and shutters. On the lawn, two seven-year-old boys in identical blue swimming trunks played beneath a water sprinkler.

"Hi, Liza," chirped her brothers Hal and Jimmy.

"Hi, twins," she teased, knowing they hated being called that.

The boys stuck out their tongues at her. She stuck out her tongue, but they were already too busy playing again to notice.

When Liza opened the front door, a blast of air conditioning wafted around her, wonderfully cold on her sweaty forehead.

In the living room, a woman in a white nurse's uniform sat in an armchair with her feet up on the matching ottoman. She had a pretty face, very much like Liza's, but older. Her thick brown hair was styled in a French braid, tucked under at the bottom.

"Mom, you wouldn't believe what happened today," Liza began.

"After a day like the one I had, I would believe anything," her mother said wearily. "But what happened?"

Breathlessly, Liza told her all about the movie, neglecting to mention her dunk in the pool. "And so I'm going to make a videotape to give to Miles Lockhart," she concluded.

"Miles Lockhart," Mrs. Velez said. "When I was a kid, *King Corral* was my favorite show."

"I can't picture you as a kid," said Liza.

"Well, believe me, I was a kid once," her mother replied. "Listen to me," she added. "You can make the video, but I want you to check with me if anything comes of it."

"Oh, something will come of it," Liza assured her. "Because this video is going to be great." Liza suddenly realized she was hungry. "What's for supper?" she asked.

"I don't know," said her mother. "Have any requests?"

"Pizza."

"Okay," Mrs. Velez said, rising slowly from her chair. "I'll call Emilio's."

"Why don't we try Flamingo Pizza?" Liza casually suggested.

"Their pizza is terrible," her mother objected.

"I like it a lot. Please . . . *please*."

Mrs. Velez shot her daughter a quizzical look. "I know you're up to something, but I'm too tired to argue. I assisted in two surgeries today."

"Thanks," Liza said, running to the kitchen to dial Flamingo Pizza, hoping Eddie would be her delivery boy.

She was struck with a pang of guilt as her mother's words came to her in a sort of delayed feedback. "Two surgeries, wow!" Liza said belatedly. "Why don't you go upstairs and lie down while I call the pizza place?"

"Sounds good," her mother replied, but before she was halfway up the stairs the doorbell rang. "See who that is, will you?" she called to Liza. "It's probably for you."

Liza opened the door and faced a tall, handsome man with dark eyes and hair. "Dad!" she cried. "Hi!" Liza's parents were divorced and Mr. Velez came to see his children every weekend. Liza wasn't that surprised to see him now, though. He often dropped by unannounced—even though it irritated her mother to no end.

Mr. Velez ruffled Liza's hair as though she were a small girl and kissed her forehead. "Hello, Sunshine," he said.

"Hello, Rick," Mrs. Velez said as he stepped into the house. Her tone was polite, but not welcoming. "What brings you here?"

"Can't a man see his own kids?" Mr. Velez asked with forced joviality.

Liza felt her shoulders tighten. She could hear the edge in both their voices. Mrs. Velez gave him a tight smile and turned back up the stairs. "Go right ahead. I'm taking a nap."

Liza relaxed a little. If her mother left, it would be okay. Her father was a great guy, as far as Liza was concerned. Her mother even agreed that in many ways he was a terrific man, but the two of them couldn't be in the same room without fighting.

"Do you think the boys should be running around outside without shoes?" Mr. Velez asked with the same jolliness as before.

"Rick, they're kids. They can go barefoot on their own lawn," Mrs. Velez snapped.

"Hey, don't get excited," her father replied. "I just don't want them to step on glass or something."

"Rick, I am the mother here. I make the rules!"

"And I'm nobody? I'm just the father. That doesn't count."

"Of course it counts," her mother said.

"I'm not so sure. I'm just the money machine around here."

"How dare you say that!" cried Mrs. Velez. "I work like a dog *and* take care of this household."

"What's this Jimmy tells me about the VCR being broken?" Mr. Velez asked. "I don't have the money to pay for a new one."

"Who asked you to?" Mrs. Velez shouted.

Liza folded her arms and drifted into the kitchen. She wasn't really upset. She'd heard this all too often. It was just that a cold sadness welled up inside her and settled like a clump in the pit of her stomach. She wished they could get along. She wished they weren't divorced, but at least now the house was peaceful . . . most of the time.

She looked at the yellow wall phone and decided not to call Flamingo Pizza. It would be too embarrassing if Eddie came and her parents were still fighting. She phoned Emilio's instead. *Well*, she thought, *at least I won't have to eat a Flamingo pizza.* Her mother was right. They were terrible.

"Look, I'm exhausted. I can't discuss this with you right now!" she heard her mother's raised voice.

"Fine. I came here to see the kids, anyway. I'll be in the front yard with the boys!" Liza heard the front door slam. And then the house was quiet.

She went into her small bedroom behind the kitchen and shut the door, glad to be in her own private haven. Liza loved her room. She'd decorated it the way she liked. The gray and yellow American Indian blanket her father had brought her from Nevada lay on her single bed, on top of bright orange sheets. She'd made a collage of her favorite stars on the window shade, and several colorful movie posters graced the walls.

She turned on her window fan and lay on the bed, gazing at her posters. She imagined a poster of herself, wearing a glamorous red dress that draped gracefully off her shoulders and was tapered down to her ankles. Her hair would fall to her waist. Her head would be thrown back and she'd be laughing. It would be easy to laugh; when she became a star, she'd be happy all the time.

Liza knew she had talent. She'd gotten the lead or

second lead in all her class plays. Of course, she loved the attention. But that wasn't what drew her to performing. When she sang, danced or acted, she felt more alive than at any other time. She loved the feeling, her heart pounding, every nerve in her body tingling.

Liza was convinced she would have been a teen star long before now if she didn't have geography working against her. If she lived in Hollywood or New York, she'd probably already be on TV. But now fate was finally on her side. Hollywood had come to Bonita Beach, come to get her.

Rolling onto her stomach, she began to dig in the jumble of softcover books under her bed. They were the scripts of plays she'd collected over the years.

"I have to find just the right one," she muttered. "This has got to be the best video Miles Lockhart has ever seen!"

Chapter Four

"Maybe we shouldn't have done this," Sam said to Chris as she hung up the wall phone in Liza's kitchen the following day. She was feeling guilty that they had just ordered a pie from Flamingo Pizza without telling Liza.

"If we tell her, she'll just get nervous," said Chris.

"Okay," Sam sighed doubtfully. "If you say so."

Chris picked up the video camera off the kitchen table and went out into the yard. The girls had the day off, and they were devoting it to shooting Liza's video. Liza had rehearsed by herself all afternoon. Now she felt ready to commit her performance to tape, with the help of Sam and Chris.

In the yard, Liza was busy tacking a pink velour blanket to the backyard fence. "This will make a good backdrop, don't you think?" she said excitedly.

"It's colorful," Sam admitted.

"I thought so, too," said Liza. "As for my performance, I'll do some dialogue, sing a song which will lead into a dance and finish with my impersonation of Grandma Kootchie."

"Oh nooooo," Chris moaned, smiling. Grandma Kootchie was a character Liza had created at a slumber party last year. She was an eccentric old lady who spoke in a high, loud voice to an invisible friend and insulted everyone. The kids they baby-sat for were always asking Liza to do Grandma.

Liza looked at the blanket dubiously. "You don't think this is going to look tacky, do you?"

"No, it's going to be framed in the camera," Chris assured her.

"I can't believe I won't be able to see this video," Liza complained. "Our stupid VCR broke."

"Come to my house," Sam suggested. "I know mine works because my sister and Lloyd were watching surfer movies on it when I left."

"Thanks," said Liza. She stood and studied her improvised set one last time. "The other actors who handed in videos probably made them in real studios."

"That's not always true," said Chris, calling upon her knowledge of trivia. "Harrison Springfield had to go to his first audition in his carpenter's overalls because he didn't have time to change."

"Harrison Springfield? Really?" Liza asked with great interest.

Chris thought about stories of other stars who had come from humble beginnings. "You know Terry Washington, the singer? She was a hairdresser. And she keeps her hairdresser's license current to this day, just in case. And Taylor Hartford—who's real name is Alice Stopplemyer—used to collect money in a self-service gas station. She sat in one of those glass booths for years before she landed a part on 'Crime Creatures.'"

Liza smiled. "I can see it now—'Liza V. was discovered while baby-sitting at the Palm Pavilion.'"

"Liza who?" asked Sam, leaning against Liza's picnic table.

"Liza V. That's what I'm thinking of calling myself."

"I thought you were going to just call yourself Liza," Sam reminded her.

"I was, but I think Liza V. sounds better. It sounds . . . I don't know, more sophisticated somehow."

"Are we going to make this video or sit around talking?" asked Chris, lifting the camera to her eye.

"One second." Liza pulled a ratty hat from a cardboard box. She yanked the elastic from her hair and let her ponytail fall loose around her shoulders. Then she took an old blanket from the box and threw it around her shoulders. "I'm a proper lady, I am," she said with a broad English cockney accent.

"Great idea!" said Chris, remembering how good Liza had been as Eliza Doolittle in *My Fair Lady*, their seventh-grade play.

"I know. And I thought it would help Miles remember my name. You know, Eliza–Liza." Liza handed Sam the script. "You read the Henry Higgins part," she told her.

"I'm not going to be in this video," Sam protested.

"Just read the lines off-camera," Liza instructed.

Sam agreed and they went through the scene. Chris taped it all as Liza spoke to the air, but then stopped the scene abruptly. "I think we should do this again from the beginning."

"Why?" asked Sam.

"Because, Liza, you keep rolling your eyes and sighing every time Sam reads a line," said Chris.

"Well, she reads them like she's reading a textbook, without any feeling," Liza said, exasperated. "Come-a-long-my-girl," she parroted Sam's flat delivery.

"You're the actress, not me!" Sam exploded.

"Can't you do it with a little feeling?" Liza shouted back.

"Hey, you guys, cut it out," said Chris. "Liza, why don't you try a part where Eliza speaks without interruption?"

"You mean the monologue?" said Liza.

"Whatever," Chris replied. She rewound the cassette and taped Liza without Sam's lines. Chris had to admit Liza had real talent. If she didn't know Liza so well, she might have believed she was the little flower peddler who was transformed into a proper English lady by Professor Higgins.

For her next act, Liza re-created the role she'd done in their eighth-grade English class, that of Juliet in *Romeo and Juliet*.

"Shakespeare should impress him," she said, braiding her hair to one side. She pulled a long pink chiffon dress with puffed sleeves from the box.

"Can you believe this was my mother's high-school

prom dress?" she laughed, with the dress over her head. She used it as a kind of dressing tent, throwing her T-shirt out the top, and then pulling it down. "How do I look?"

Chris exchanged glances with Sam. "I think your mother had a little more on top than you do," said Sam.

Liza looked down ruefully at the dress, which sagged around her rib cage. "No problem," she said, reaching into the box once again. She took out a wadded-up pair of socks and stuck one balled-up sock in each side of the dress. "Better?"

"Much!" Chris giggled.

Liza turned to Sam. "I am *not* being Romeo. No way," Sam insisted, jumping off the picnic table and backing away.

"I just want you to read along and make sure I don't forget any lines," Liza told her. She handed Sam the script and then stepped in front of the blanket.

Chris focused in on Liza once again as Liza pretended she was Juliet standing alone on her balcony in the moonlight, talking about her love for Romeo.

Usually, Chris thought Shakespeare was a pain— much too hard to read. And who cared, anyhow, about a bunch of people who lived a zillion years ago and talked funny. But when Liza spoke the lines, they made sense to Chris for the first time. Juliet was a girl who was madly in love with a boy, just like any girl today.

Liza finished the scene and changed clothing again.

This time she wore her own clothes—black stretch pants, a long yellow top and lots of bracelets. She put her hair into a ponytail at the top of her head. She sang the Beatles song, "Help," without accompaniment.

Finally it was time for Grandma Kootchie. Liza ran into the house and emerged five minutes later wearing a white synthetic wig, which Chris remembered from several Halloweens past. She had on a long, baggy dress and carried a big stick as a cane.

Chris aimed the camera at her. "It's Grandma Kootchie time!" Liza bellowed in a high, scratchy voice. "Hey, Lavinia," she said to her imaginary friend. "What do you say to a three-headed monster? Hello. Hello. Hello." Liza stepped up on top of the picnic table. Chris followed her with the camera. "You know, Lavinia, I met old Doc Parsons the other day. I said, 'Doc, I wish I had the money to come see you every week.' 'Why? Is something wrong with you, Grandma?' he asked. I said, 'No, you fool. I just wish I had that much money.'"

Chris and Sam groaned but laughed despite themselves. "Now I'm going to do a little foot stompin' dance for you all," Liza spoke into the camera. Chris grinned. She'd seen Liza do this dance. It actually required some fancy footwork. It only looked ridiculous because everything about Grandma Kootchie was goofy.

Liza lifted her dress and revealed a pair of high-button shoes with mismatched socks bunched at the ankles. She bent and turned as the wail of country violins filled the air. Then she began hopping about on the table, moving her feet at almost lightning speed.

30

Stomping hard on the wooden table, Liza turned and hopped through the air. She spun around twice, and then, suddenly—through the lens of the camera—Chris saw Liza stop abruptly, a horrified look spreading across her face.

Chris whirled around to see what Liza was looking at. Standing at the back gate, holding a pizza, was Eddie.

"How long have you been there?" gasped Liza.

"Long enough, Grandma Kootchie," he laughed. "Long enough."

Chapter Five

Liza stood at her front screen door the next morning and looked out. The air was still and she could already feel that it was going to be a scorcher. She wondered if Hollywood was as hot as southern Florida. *It certainly couldn't be any hotter*, she told herself.

Chris would be arriving any minute to ride to work with her. Liza hadn't decided yet whether or not she was still mad at Chris and Sam. On the one hand, she had been mortified when Eddie showed up. But on the other, he did laugh and seem to think it was funny. He even stuck around a few minutes to talk, though he had to get back to work. He was so nice, and he seemed to have a good sense of humor. Still, her Grandma Kootchie getup was hardly the outfit she wanted to be seen in. *Why couldn't Eddie have come during Juliet?* she wondered.

To be fair, though, Sam and Chris didn't even know she was going to do Grandma Kootchie. And they hadn't intended to be mean. *Okay, so I'm not all that mad,* she admitted to herself.

Liza glanced at her watch. It was almost eight o'clock. Chris usually arrived by ten to eight. She suddenly worried that maybe Chris had taken her at her word and wasn't coming at all.

Sitting back on the stoop, Liza waited a few more minutes. Just when she was beginning to think she'd have to ride to work alone, she saw Chris and Sam coming up the block. That was unusual because they always picked up Sam last. "How come you picked up Sam first?" she asked Chris.

"I wasn't coming here by myself," Chris answered. "Not after the way you acted yesterday."

Liza pressed her lips together and looked at them. She folded her arms. "Say you're sorry," she said.

"Oh, come on," Sam said irritably. "We said we were sorry a hundred times yesterday. We didn't know you were going to have that stupid outfit on."

"Yeah, well, when you saw me put it on you should have warned me!" Liza shouted.

"We forgot all about him. Honestly," said Sam.

"It was a stupid thing to do," said Chris. "Sam didn't even want to go along with it."

"It's true," said Sam, "and I got stuck paying for that crummy, dried-out pizza."

"I said I'd pay you back when we get paid Friday," said Chris. "Did anyone at least eat the pizza, Liza?"

"The twins will eat anything," Liza said, laughing. "But after they ate almost the whole thing, Jimmy patted his stomach and said, 'Don't buy that pizza again. It was disgusting.'"

"Are you coming, or what?" asked Sam.

"I guess so," said Liza, relieved not to be angry at her friends anymore. She got her bike and they headed for the hotel.

When they arrived at the Palm Pavilion, the film crew at the front entrance had already begun to shoot a scene from Miles Lockhart's movie. The three girls locked their bikes together, and Liza immediately ran toward the front of the hotel. "We're going to be late," Sam cried from behind her, but Liza couldn't help herself. She had to see what was happening on that set.

A crowd had gathered at the entrance to the hotel. Miles Lockhart and Luna Collins stood on the low, sloping steps leading into the hotel as a rain and wind machine buffeted them with a fake storm. "What's going on?" Liza asked a young, balding man wearing Bermuda shorts and holding a black slate clipboard.

"Miles and Luna are escaping from the hotel, which is being destroyed by a hurricane of mysterious origin," he explained without taking his eyes off the action. Luna Collins had on a sequinned gown with a man's trench coat thrown alluringly over her bare shoulders. Miles wore a white tuxedo, which was drenched.

"Cut! Cut!" Miles shouted, breaking out of character. The rain and wind instantly subsided. "I want a storm here," he shouted at the machine operators. "This is more like an afternoon drizzle. The title of this movie is *Alien Wind,* not *Martian Mud Puddle!* I want a storm, for heaven's sake."

"Isn't he strong and decisive?" Liza breathed as Chris and Sam each grabbed one of her arms and dragged her away from the scene.

"So is Mr. Parker," said Sam. "And after the other day, he may strongly decide to fire us if we're late.".

Liza allowed herself to be hurried along, still in a half-dream. She imagined herself in a sequinned dress being pelted with fake rain. Sheer heaven. . . .

Inside the hotel, the clatter in the kitchen shook Liza from her reverie as the girls found their time cards and punched in. It was already eight thirty-five, but thankfully Mr. Parker was not around.

Outside in the lobby, they spotted Jannette Sansibar, one of the other baby sitters. "There's Miss Perky, already at the assignment board," said Chris snidely. As they approached, Jannette gave them one of her phony, toothy smiles.

"How was your vacation?" Sam inquired politely.

"Just terrific, thanks," Jannette said. She turned to Chris. "Bruce said he saw you bright and early the other day. Jogging off those extra pounds?" she asked, still smiling.

"Yes, I mean no. I mean—"

"It's an excellent idea," Jannette cut her off. "I think I'll start going to the beach on my mornings off, too."

"Great," Liza said, flatly.

"'Jogging off a few pounds,'" Sam echoed disgustedly when the girl was out of earshot.

"I don't believe this," Chris gasped, ignoring Sam, as she checked her assignment. "I'm taking care of Luna Collins's kid, Starshine."

35

"What kind of weird name is that?" asked Sam.

"No weirder than Luna," Chris pointed out.

"That's great!" cried Liza. "See if the kid knows what room Miles Lockhart is in. Find out everything you can from her."

"It says she's three," said Chris, looking back at the assignment sheet. "I don't think she'll exactly be a gold mine of information."

"See what you can find out, anyway," Liza insisted.

"Doesn't it seem a little odd that Parker gave me this assignment?" said Chris. "I mean, this is an important kid, and I'm not his most trusted employee—to put it mildly."

"It does seem odd," Sam agreed. She found her name on the sheet. "Well, I guess I'm not getting a movie star's kid today. 'Robbie Harris' sounds like an average, everyday five-year-old to me."

Liza scanned the assignment sheet and smiled when she saw her name. "Allll right! House service! I'll have no trouble finding which room Miles is in. It's all on the house plan behind the hospitality desk."

The girls went their separate ways. Sam and Chris headed out to the pool where they were meeting their little charges and Liza went to see Mr. Halpern, the house manager, at his desk in the lobby. She had only to look over his shoulder to get a peek at the hotel's elaborate room plan.

"Seventeen-B," Liza whispered to herself, when she spotted the actor's name on the chart. "Seventeen-B, Seventeen-B." She definitely wouldn't forget it.

House service was usually a cushy job with lots of free time. Today was different, and Liza was up and down in the elevators delivering this and that—golf balls from the pro shop, coloring books from the gift shop, sunscreen and sunglasses from the hotel drugstore.

When she delivered bottles of club soda to Raoul Smith, the bartender in the Parrot Lounge on the balcony, he thanked her with a piña colada minus the alcohol. The lounge was empty as Liza sat at a small table and sipped from the tall, frosty glass. "What's it like to serve all the famous people who come here?" she asked Raoul, who was busy hanging long-stemmed glasses upside down in a wooden overhead rack.

"No big deal," he said, giving her one of his dimpled smiles. Liza could see why a lot of the girls who worked at the Palm were crazy about Raoul. He was handsome and flirted with all the females, young and old. "They're just people like you and me," he added.

"No way," said Liza. "Everything about them is different. They even look different from ordinary people."

"Oh, yeah?" said Raoul, sounding amused. "In what way?"

Scrunching her brow thoughtfully, Liza considered the question. The famous people she'd seen at the hotel were better-looking somehow. They seemed larger than life, as though they were royalty. They were wrapped in an aura of charm and grace that colored everything they did.

"Famous people are magical," Liza answered him.

Raoul chuckled wickedly. "I've seen a lot of them look pretty human here at the bar. When they drink too much, some of them act sub-human. Believe me, kiddo, they just seem better than us because they have a lot of money. Hey, I'd look great if I were wearing a five-hundred-dollar shirt right now. So would you if—"

Glancing over her shoulder, he cut himself short. "Hand over the glass, fast," he whispered quickly. "Parker."

Liza jumped up and handed him the glass just as Mr. Parker appeared on the top step of the balcony. He sighed deeply. "Miss Velez, what are you doing in the—"

"I asked her to take this wine to Chef Alleyne," said Raoul, holding up a cold bottle of white wine. "He needs it for his world-famous sole in white wine sauce." He handed Liza the bottle. "Better hurry before the chef throws one of his world-famous tantrums."

Mr. Parker eyed them skeptically. "Miss Velez, I can't help but suspect that there has been a certain amount of dawdling here, and the lounge is certainly no place—"

"Yes, sir," said Liza. "I've got to get this to Chef Alleyne. You know how he gets."

"Indeed I do," said Mr. Parker. "Get going, then."

Liza delivered the bottle to Chef Alleyne, who was surprised but glad to receive it. He didn't let Liza leave until she had given him her opinion of his new key lime pie. "French-style, of course," he noted.

Liza ate two slices just to be sure and then pronounced

the pie to be *magnifique*. This pleased Chef Alleyne so much that he offered her another piece, but she was too full to accept it.

Liza was having fun, but still, she couldn't wait for her shift to end. She had to get that tape to 17-B.

Finally, one o'clock came and her shift was over. She spotted Chris and Sam coming across the lobby. They looked sunburned and tired. Sam's child had obviously been picked up already, but Chris still had a little girl by the hand.

Starshine Collins! Liza had to meet her. *Maybe she can give me some inside scoop about the movie*, she said to herself as she hurried over, anxious to get a look at the daughter of the famous actress. "Hi," she greeted the girl enthusiastically. "I'm Liza." The girl looked up at her with angelic, round blue eyes. A mop of tousled curls surrounded her pretty face. "You look like Shirley Temple," said Liza.

"I am not Shirley Temple! Stop saying that! Stop it! Stop it! Stop it!" shrieked the girl, pulling away from Chris. She threw herself on the blue-tiled floor and kicked frantically.

Liza looked at Chris with panicked eyes. "Mr. Parker's revenge," Chris quipped. "Charming, isn't she?"

"Everybody is looking at us," Sam whispered urgently. It was true. People upstairs in the Parrot Lounge were hanging over the railing, looking to see what was causing the commotion. And the entire line of people at the check-in desk had turned to see what was going on.

"Come on, Starshine, get up," Chris coaxed, attempting to lift the girl from under the armpits.

"Nooooooo!" she wailed hysterically. Three white-haired ladies sitting together on the high-backed chairs nearby clucked and shook their heads.

"Parker is going to show up any second," said Sam.

Liza searched her pockets and pulled out a wrapped square of pink bubble gum. "Want some gum, Starshine?"

There was instant silence. Starshine hopped to her feet. "Give me," she said, extending a small, pudgy hand. Except for her wet eyelashes, there was no sign that she had ever been upset.

"What do you say?" Liza asked before handing over the gum.

"Give me."

"No, that's not what you say. Come on now—"

"Just give her the darn gum, will you?" Sam snapped. "Here comes her mother."

"There's my angel!" gushed Luna Collins, coming toward them with her arms wide open. "Did my ootsy-wootsy have a good time today?"

Starshine ran to her mother. "She no let me dive off the big board," Starshine complained, pointing an accusing finger at Chris.

Luna Collins, still in the sequinned gown, tossed back her mane of permed blond hair. "Starshine is into everything. You simply cannot hold her down," she trilled. "Someday, you're going to be a star, just like Mommy. I know you are." Her face suddenly grew serious. "You didn't have any trouble with her, did you?"

40

"Oh, she was fine," Chris lied.

"Her nanny needed a vacation and my dear, dear friend Harrison Springfield told me you were so good with his little Jason when he was here, that I told that delightful Mr. Parker I absolutely had to have you take care of my little sweetheart."

"Oh, uh, thanks," said Chris, not quite sure how to take this news.

Luna Collins picked up her daughter and headed back out of the lobby. "We'll see you tomorrow!" she called over her shoulder.

Chris waved, a sickly grin on her face. "Oh, man!" she moaned. "Not again tomorrow. That kid is a nightmare! She should be called Witchinghour, not Starshine. I had to drag her off the diving board, kicking and screaming, five times. Then she jumped into the deep end of the pool."

"She's a good swimmer?" asked Liza.

"No. She's a maniac!" Chris cried. "She can't swim a stroke. She just doesn't know the meaning of the word fear. I had to jump in after her, and the lifeguard bawled me out for ten minutes."

"I don't envy you," said Sam sympathetically.

"I don't envy me either," said Chris. "I'm going straight home and into bed. I'm exhausted. I need at least fifteen hours of sleep."

"Sorry," said Liza. "No beddy-bye for you yet."

"Why? What?" Chris muttered pitifully. "I don't even have the strength to ride my bike home. Will one of you carry me?"

41

"Hang in there a little longer," said Liza. "You're going to stand guard while I go up to Miles Lockhart's room."

"Why me?" Chris whimpered, covering her eyes with her hands.

"See ya," said Sam, heading across the lobby.

"Oh, no you don't!" Liza grabbed her by the sleeve of her polo shirt. "I need both of you to help me. Here's my plan. . . ."

Chapter Six

"Remember," Liza called through the closing elevator door to Sam and Chris out in the lobby. "Ring the house phone three times if someone is coming." She had assigned Chris to stand guard near the express elevator and Sam to be on the lookout farther up the hall. They would ring her three times if someone was coming up to suite 17-B.

Liza pushed back her hair and straightened her Palm Pavilion polo shirt. She had to look calm and official, since she wasn't sure what she was going to encounter when she knocked on the door of 17-B.

She clutched the bottle of sparkling water she'd talked Raoul into selling her. If someone was in the suite, she'd pretend she was delivering it, compliments of the hotel. Wrapped in a white bar cloth was her video. She would lay it down next to the bottle and leave—but not before she'd casually removed the cloth.

When the elevator door opened, Liza cautiously stuck

her head into the hallway. She was in luck. Two chamber maids were on the floor, and all the doors were wide open.

Liza stepped into the hallway and quickly looked inside the suites. "They're so beautiful," she sighed. There were four suites on each VIP floor, and they all faced the ocean. They each had a living room, kitchenette and dining room—not to mention two to six bedrooms. Plate glass windows and sliding glass doors lined the walls.

Liza peeked into 17-B. The maid's cart stood in the center of the living room but the suite was empty. She heard a noise coming from 17-D. The maid was working in there, she assumed.

Cautiously, she stepped into 17-B, which was decorated in a chic deep green with white leather furnishings. She was about to lay her video on the glass end table when she had a brainstorm. She went to the VCR, turned the power on, then slipped the video into the slot and set the TV channel for VCR. It was perfect. As soon as Miles Lockhart turned on the set, he would see that something was in the VCR. He'd have to be curious about what it was.

Satisfied that she'd accomplished her mission, Liza turned toward the door and saw a batch of color photos on the desk across the room. Miles Lockhart's private snapshots! She'd never have this chance again—she had to see them!

Checking over her shoulder, Liza hurried across the room. She picked up the pictures and her jaw dropped.

The pictures showed Miles with his arms around Tara Harold, the actress who starred in *Eagle Valley*, a show about the adventures of park rangers who were always falling in love with one another. But Tara Harold was supposed to be engaged to Russ Mason, her co-star. At least that's what Liza had read in the *World Tattler* magazine, which was supposed to have the inside scoop on all the stars.

Liza smiled. She, Liza Velez, had outscooped the *Tattler*. Chris would faint when she found out.

A sudden urge made Liza wrestle with her conscience. Could she sneak just one little picture from the batch? Just to show Chris and Sam? Miles wouldn't miss it— unless she took his favorite shot. No, she'd have to leave them behind.

She flipped through the photos one more time. She realized they'd been taken in Paris, with the Eiffel Tower in the background. Liza sighed and wondered if she'd ever get to Paris. *Maybe someday I'll make a movie there*, she thought, hopefully. *I can just see it. I'll star as a member of the French underground during World War Two, passing secrets about Nazi activity.*

Liza imagined herself wearing a lavender flowered scarf over her head and meeting a mysterious agent in a small café. She'd pass him a paper and he'd clutch her hand. Then he'd tell her of his love. "Our time is short, Pierre," Liza whispered aloud to the fantasy spy. "Already the clock is chiming. One, two, three." Liza felt as if she could really hear the bells.

But wait. There it was again. One. Two. Three! She *had* heard bells!

45

Liza's eyes widened. That was no clock! That was the house phone. She raced across the room. "Hello?"

"What took you so long?" scolded Sam on the other end. "Get out of there. Parker's already in the express elevator."

Liza slammed down the phone and bolted for the door. The fire stairs! That's how she'd leave. She might have to walk down seventeen flights, but anything was better than being caught by sourpuss Parker.

But Liza was too late. The light above the elevator was already blinking. Any second now, the door would open and she'd be staring into Mr. Parker's icy eyes.

She looked around frantically in all directions. There was no place to go. She was trapped!

Then she noticed the maid's cart. Without thinking, she ran over and climbed into it, pulling the used sheets over her head. The strong smell of a man's cologne surrounded her. Even though her heart was pounding with fear, she was thrilled to be covered with a sheet smelling of Miles Lockhart's cologne.

Within seconds she heard Mr. Parker's familiar bellow. "Now what seems to be the problem up here?"

"It's in Seventeen-B," Liza heard the maid answer. Liza recognized Betty's voice. Betty was one of the old-time maids who'd been with the hotel since it had opened twenty-five years ago.

Mr. Parker and Betty—what a nightmare team! Liza thought despairingly. Betty acted like she owned the place, and Mr. Parker—was Mr. Parker. Liza pulled the sheet farther over her head.

"The leak is in the bedroom," Betty said, standing next to the cart. "It's ruining the wallpaper and the rug."

Mr. Parker let out a prolonged, agonized sigh. "It's always something. Always something in this hotel. Let me see this."

When their voices drifted into the bedroom, Liza dared to peer out of the cart. The coast was clear. She'd bolt for the fire exit and pray for the best.

"Just my luck!" Mr. Parker exploded, causing Liza to duck back into the cart. "My most famous guest gets the one room with a leaky bedroom ceiling. Of course, it's wildly optimistic of me to think this is the only room with a leak. No doubt, all the rooms will soon spring leaks. And all because I have a movie crew and a convention of chicken salespeople to attend to."

"I haven't seen any other leaks," Betty assured him.

"No, no, of course not," said Mr. Parker sarcastically. They had come out of the bedroom now and were standing right next to the cart. Liza clapped her hands over her mouth so they wouldn't hear her breathing.

"Let me think about this. I have to do something quickly," Mr. Parker grumbled.

Liza heard him walk toward the door. *They're leaving*, she thought. *I've done it. I'm going to get out of this in one piece.*

But suddenly Liza was jostled. Betty was trying to roll the cart out of the room—and it wouldn't budge!

"What's wrong?" inquired Mr. Parker from the door.

"Darn cart won't move. The wheels are stuck," Betty told him.

47

"Here, let me help," said Mr. Parker. Liza was jolted repeatedly, as he kicked the wheels a few times. "Try it now," he said.

Betty jiggled the cart. "This is the strangest . . ." she muttered. The next thing Liza knew, the sweet cologne-scented sheet was lifted off her head and she was staring up into Betty's surprised green eyes.

Chapter Seven

"Yes indeed, you've fixed it, Mr. Parker," said Betty. "I can always count on you."

"Very good then, I'll be off," said Mr. Parker.

Liza couldn't believe it. Betty—Miss Palm Pavilion herself—was covering for her. She hunched down in the cart, not wanting to blow the whole thing by getting up before Mr. Parker left.

The suite door closed and then Betty gave the cart a little shake. "All right, get up," she scolded. Liza stood up and sheepishly faced the small, wiry woman with short, curly white hair. "Now let's hear it," Betty demanded. "And it better be good."

"Thank you, Betty, for not turning me in. I would have been fired." Liza said as she climbed out of the cart.

"And what were you doing up here?" Betty demanded.

Liza had to think fast. Betty would be furious if she told her about the video. "I just wanted to see Miles

49

Lockhart's room. He's my favorite actor. I swear I didn't touch anything."

"You better not have." Betty frowned. "I won't be blamed for stealing. If anything is gone from this room, I'll report you."

"I understand, Betty, but nothing's missing, honestly," Liza said as she headed for the door. "Thank you again."

Betty winked. "I wasn't born this old, you know. I know how it is to be enamored of a movie star. But if anything's gone from this room—even a comb you took as a memento—put it back now."

"It's all here, I promise," Liza repeated. Giving Betty a quick smile, she headed out the door. *I'll take the stairs*, she figured. It was stupid to take the chance of running into Mr. Parker if he was coming back up just as she was going down.

She opened the fire door and ran down the first five flights of stairs. Feeling winded, she tried the door at the twelfth floor landing to see if she could take the local elevator from there, but it was locked. In fact, all the floor entrances, except on the top and bottom floors, were locked from the outside. Seventeen flights later, Liza emerged into the hall, panting from the effort, her hair plastered to the side of her face with perspiration.

She spotted Chris and Sam standing in the lobby, looking around anxiously. "Boo!" she said, sneaking up behind them.

Both girls jumped. "Boo yourself. What happened?" asked Sam.

"Mission accomplished," Liza said triumphantly.

"You avoided Parker?" asked Chris.

"Thanks to Betty," said Liza. "I'll tell you about it on the way home." As they left the hotel together Liza filled them in on the whole story and then told Chris about the photos of Miles and Tara.

"Wow! Maybe we should call a magazine and tell them," Chris suggested. "They might pay for info like that."

"No way," Sam warned. "Parker would do a double flip in the air and turn green and definitely fire you."

"If you were lucky," added Liza.

When Liza got home she checked the phone-answering machine hoping for a message from Eddie. He hadn't said he would call, but she was hoping anyway. She could tell he liked her, but she didn't know anything about him. She'd have to find a way to ask Bruce if he was already going with someone.

That night Liza could hardly sleep. Tomorrow would be the big day. Miles would find the video and see her. She tried to imagine the expression on his face. Awe? Excitement? Horror?

No, not horror. The tape was good. She'd put her phone number on the video, but hopefully he'd spot her at the hotel even before he called. *I'll know if he liked it the minute I see his face*, she told herself. Rolling toward the wall, she pulled her sheet over her head, but couldn't fall asleep. "Aaaaaaahhhh," she growled with frustration and rolled back out to the edge of the bed, hanging her head off the side. Would this night ever end?

At about twelve, she gave up on sleep and turned her light back on. She picked up the copy of *Persons* which lay at her bedside and began leafing through it. She was distracted though, still trying to picture the look on Miles Lockhart's face when he saw her video. Finally, she dozed off.

The next day Liza got up early to wash her hair and put on a little eye makeup and some coral-colored lipstick. She had to look just right when she spoke to Miles Lockhart.

She was ready a full half hour before Chris came by. "Why isn't she here yet?" Liza muttered, rapping her spoon anxiously against her juice glass as she sat at the kitchen table.

"Relax," said her mother, pouring herself coffee. "I have patients who are calmer about going into surgery than you are now."

"Well good for them," snapped Liza irritably.

"Liza, take a deep breath, please," said her mother.

There was a rap at the front door and Liza ran to answer it.

"Good luck," her mother called as Liza let the front door slam.

"It's about time," Liza greeted Chris.

"Good morning to you, too," said Chris. "And, for your information, I'm exactly on time."

"Okay, sorry. Let's go," said Liza, wheeling her bike out from the side of the house. She hopped on and they rode together to pick up Sam. When the three of them arrived at the Palm Pavilion, there was no sign of the movie crew. "What if they left?" Liza gasped.

Sam and Chris looked at her with worried expressions. "I never thought of that," said Sam.

"Maybe they're here somewhere," said Chris hopefully.

They felt relieved when they stepped out of the kitchen and into the hotel restaurant. The place was flooded with lights all focusing on a small, elegantly set table where Miles Lockhart and Luna Collins were seated.

"Look," Liza said, pointing to a tall, slim waiter wearing a tuxedo and taking the actors' orders. "Gene is in the movie."

They watched as he wrote in his pad, smiled, nodded and walked off the set. "Gene," Liza said as she rushed up to the man, who really was a waiter in the restaurant. "How did you get into the movie?"

Gene laughed. "Some of us have star quality, I suppose," he teased in his lilting island accent. "Plus, I am the early set-up man today, and I suppose they liked the tuxedo."

"The right place at the right time," said Liza. "What luck! That's how it all starts."

"Well, I don't think I'll be packing for Hollywood just yet," said Gene.

"You never can tell. Stranger things have happened."

Gene chuckled and walked away. "I think maybe you should wipe those stars from your eyes," he called to Liza as he pushed in the kitchen door.

"The man has one of the greatest experiences of his life, and he doesn't even appreciate it," Liza muttered.

She hovered around the lights for a few minutes, trying to catch Miles Lockhart's attention. "Hey, watch it," said a camera man when Liza accidentally walked into him. The disturbance distracted Miles, who peered into the lights and squinted.

Suddenly, two hands reached out and grabbed Liza by the shoulders. "Come on," said Chris, pulling Liza along.

"Do you think he winked at me?" Liza asked. "I couldn't tell through the glare of the lights."

"He was trying to see who was messing up his scene," Chris pointed out.

"No, he might have winked," Liza insisted. "I'm not sure."

When the girls got out into the lobby, there was an unusually large crowd of people. A big sign read, "Welcome Plucky Chicken Sales Force." Men and women were milling about, holding their suitcases and talking to one another.

"Plucky Chicken," said Sam. "Isn't that the company whose owner says in a TV commercial that he personally inspects every chicken he sells?"

"Yeah, that tall, skinny guy with glasses and red curly hair," Chris confirmed. "I wonder if he'll be here."

"Miles Lockhart and Luna Collins are here, and you're excited about seeing Mr. Plucky Chicken," said Liza with disdain.

"He's on TV," Chris defended herself. "That makes him famous."

"I suppose," said Liza with a shrug.

As they stood watching the commotion in the lobby,

the movie crew behind them left the restaurant and headed out into the lobby.

"There you are, dear," said Luna Collins to Chris. "I'll bring Starshine to meet you at the front desk. She's been rehearsing a song to sing for you."

"How cute." Chris barely smiled. "I guess I don't have to check the bulletin board," she griped when the woman had gone.

"Lucky you," said Liza. "That kid makes Attila the Hun look like—" Liza cut herself short. Miles Lockhart was coming right toward her. She smiled brightly at him.

He returned her smile. Then he raised his thumb and index finger in the shape of a gun and pointed at her as he winked.

Liza's heart started to race. She opened her mouth to speak, but he kept on walking. She stood there looking at Chris and Sam.

"That was definitely a wink," breathed Chris, "and a point."

"But why didn't he stop?" asked Sam.

"Maybe he was in a hurry," Chris suggested.

"He saw the video, I know it," whispered Liza, her hand over her pounding heart. "He loved it. I'm going to be in the movie!"

Chapter Eight

"Pay attention to the board!" snapped the old man. "Your head is in the clouds today."

"Sorry, Mr. Schwartz," said Liza. "I guess I was thinking about something else. . . . What did you say?"

"I just did a triple jump while you were daydreaming," he replied. "I know you let me win, but you take all the fun out of the game when you're so ridiculously obvious about it."

Liza didn't know what to say. "Well, maybe sometimes," she stammered.

"You're not yourself today," he cut her off. "What's the matter?"

"Nothing's the matter. Just the opposite," she said. Usually, she talked very little to Mr. Schwartz. They played checkers and that was about it. But today Liza was bubbling over with enthusiasm. She was glad to have the chance to tell him about getting into Miles Lockhart's movie. She wanted to tell the whole world.

"So, did this Lockhart fellow tell you that you were in?" Mr. Schwartz asked skeptically.

"No," Liza admitted, "but you should have seen the look he gave me. I'm sure he'll tell me soon. He was probably just in a hurry at the time."

"Well, then, good luck to you. I can tell you it's a tough business."

"You can?" Liza asked, surprised. How would old Mr. Schwartz know?

"I was only in the business for seventy years. Started as an extra when I was fifteen. I did it all. Silents. Musicals. In fact, I was in the audience behind Al Jolson when he made the first big talkie."

"You were?" Liza gasped.

"Sure. Then I did stunt work for many years, with an occasional talking part. I played thugs, robbers, and every so often I was a cowboy."

Liza couldn't picture this shriveled, cranky old man riding a horse, let alone performing stunts. She took a closer look at his watery blue eyes, the transparent skin that showed all his veins and his high, bony cheekbones, and for the first time she tried to imagine what he once looked like. It occurred to her that he might even have been handsome when he was young.

"It's a cutthroat business," Mr. Schwartz went on. "I married three times because I let work be more important than anything else—I was always dreaming that I'd be the next John Wayne, always trying to be in the right place at the right time. I even changed my name. Back then I was known as Chas Reynolds. Ever hear of him?"

Liza shook her head. "Maybe my friend Chris has heard of you," she said, trying to be nice. "She knows a lot of trivia about famous people."

"I'm not one of them, I can assure you," he said wistfully. "It wasn't a bad life, though. I made a good penny for an unknown, a very good penny. I stay at this hotel, don't I?"

"So you don't regret anything?" Liza ventured.

"I regret a lot. I regret having no wife, no children. I regret that I'm the only one who can spot me in my movies."

"I'd love to see you," said Liza sincerely. "Let me know the next time one of your movies is on TV and tell me where to look for you."

Mr. Schwartz fixed her with a quizzical stare. "Are you really interested?"

"Sure I am. I think it's very exciting that you were in movies. Did you ever meet John Wayne?"

Mr. Schwartz settled back in his chair. "I've met all of them."

"Who did you like best?" Liza asked.

Mr. Schwartz leaned forward on his bony elbows. Forgetting about their half-finished checkers game, he began telling Liza stories of all the famous stars he'd worked with. Liza was fascinated. It was like traveling back in a time machine to the early days of Hollywood. And Mr. Schwartz had lots of funny stories to tell. She'd never realized he had a sense of humor.

The time passed quickly. Liza didn't realize it was one o'clock until she noticed Chris, looking frazzled, carrying a screaming Starshine Collins under her arm. "Thanks for telling me those stories," Liza told Mr. Schwartz as she gathered up the checkers pieces. "You've had an interesting life."

"It has been interesting," Mr. Schwartz agreed. The old, cranky expression returned to his face. "And next time I want you to play me a real game of checkers," he said.

"Okay," Liza smiled at him. "Wish me luck with Miles Lockhart."

"Good luck."

Liza left him and joined Chris just in time to see Starshine bite her leg. "Ouch!" Chris yelped.

The little girl spotted Liza. "Gum!" she demanded. "I want gum."

"I don't have any today," said Liza.

Starshine let out a howl. "She's been like this all day," moaned Chris, rubbing her leg. "I'm exhausted."

Liza laid the checkers on the floor. "Here, Starshine," she said. "Why don't you stack all the checkers and see how high you can pile them?"

Starshine sniffed and considered the idea. Without a word, she sat down on the lobby floor and began the task.

Sam arrived, looking happy. "Guess what I did today?" she said.

"I give up," Chris said, flopping down onto one of the soft green chairs that dotted the lobby.

"There was no baby-sitting for me, so I caddied for Hank Halliday."

"Who's he?" asked Liza.

"He's the Plucky Chicken guy from TV. He really does own the company. He told me that he makes his sales-people come to a convention here—even though nobody wants to come to Florida in the summer—because he loves the golf course."

"Nice guy," said Chris sarcastically. "Well, there sure are enough salespeople wandering around the hotel all of a sudden," she commented.

"Yeah, and none of them brought their kids," said Sam. "It's going to be slow for us until this convention is over."

"I wish Luna Collins hadn't brought her kid," Chris whispered. As she spoke, Chris looked down casually at Starshine—just in time to see her shoot a red checker across the way, hitting a man on the top of his bald head.

"Sorry," Chris apologized to the man. But she wasn't fast enough to stop Starshine from sending a black checker whizzing past a woman's nose.

"Stop that," Chris scolded, trying to pry the checkers from Starshine's clenched fists.

"I want my checkers!" Starshine screamed hysterically. "I want my checkers!"

Liza spotted Luna Collins coming toward them. And Miles Lockhart was with her! *He's coming to talk to me!* thought Liza excitedly. *This is it!* "Quiet, Starshine, sweetie," she whispered urgently. She didn't want this little kid ruining her big moment.

Miles Lockhart was only a few paces away when Mrs. Chan, the petite woman in charge of the front desk, beckoned to Liza from behind the registration desk. Mrs. Chan was very nice, but she wasn't someone you kept waiting. She was second in charge after Mr. Parker.

Liza's eyes darted anxiously from Miles Lockhart to Mrs. Chan. She couldn't leave now. Not when Miles was going to tell her how much he loved her video.

"Keep them talking," she said to Chris and Sam.

"About what?" snapped Chris, trying to calm down the still-screaming Starshine.

"Anything. Tell them what a delightful child Starshine is. Just don't let them get away!" Checking back over her shoulder every few seconds, Liza rushed over to see what Mrs. Chan wanted.

"Liza, dear, would you please take this bottle of champagne up to Miles Lockhart's room before you leave?" Mrs. Chan asked.

"He's right over there. I'll give it to him," Liza suggested. *This is perfect!* she thought gleefully. *It gives me a reason to go talk to Miles.*

"No, don't give it to him. He doesn't want to carry it. That's why he asked us to deliver it," said Mrs. Chan. "He's in Sixteen-C. Some of the movie crew are up there now."

"You mean Seventeen-B," Liza corrected her.

"No, there was a leak in Seventeen-B, so Mr. Parker switched Mr. Lockhart to Sixteen-C."

Liza's jaw dropped. "When did he do that?"

"Yesterday after the maids finished the rooms," Mrs. Chan explained, handing her the cold bottle of champagne.

"You mean last night Miles Lockhart slept in Sixteen-C?" Liza asked, clutching the bottle tensely by its neck.

"That's right," Mrs. Chan said. "Does that bother you for some reason?"

Liza forced her gaping mouth shut. "No, not at all," she stammered.

That meant Miles hadn't seen her video, after all, she realized. He'd just smiled at her to be friendly. Maybe he remembered her from when she fell into the pool—remembered her as a goofy, klutzy kid. *This is terrible!* she thought miserably.

Her hopes dashed, Liza fought back tears. What a fool she'd been to think that, because he smiled at her, he wanted her for his movie. Liza turned away from Mrs. Chan, feeling disappointed and embarrassed. Despite her efforts to stay calm, one hot tear rolled down Liza's cheek. She stooped and pretended to tie her shoelace so no one would see her crying.

Then another thought occurred to her. Who did have her video? *Maybe it's not too late if I can get it back*, she thought hopefully. She stood up and wiped any smudged makeup from under her eyes. She wasn't sure how to go about it, but she was determined to get that video back. She had to do it—and right away.

Chapter Nine

"I don't know why I always let you talk me into these things," Sam complained as the express elevator took them to the seventeenth floor. "I never ever learn my lesson. Never, never, never."

"Stop moaning and practice looking friendly," ordered Liza. "We're supposed to be a hospitality committee." Pretending to be a hospitality committee would give them an excuse to get into the room. If the video wasn't in sight, she'd pretend to check the VCR and look for her video there.

"Hello, sir. We're the Perky Hospitality Committee here to check on the service at this hotel," Chris practiced, a phony smile on her face. "Are your faucets flowing, your potted palms growing, your air conditioners blowing? Hmmmmmmmmmm?"

"You'd better not say that," Liza told Chris seriously. "They'll think you're nuts."

"I wasn't going to," Chris said. "Relax. I was just kidding."

"Sorry," Liza apologized. "I don't have a sense of humor right now. I have to get that video back."

"I don't understand why you don't just knock on the door and ask for it," said Sam.

"Because you never know how people are. They might get annoyed that I was in their room and complain to Parker."

As Liza spoke the elevator door opened. The girls got out and stood in front of 17-B. "Okay, stand up straight and look official," Liza ordered as she rapped briskly on the door.

"Yes?" asked a small woman with a head of tight, snow-white curls as she opened the door. For a moment no one spoke. The girls stood smiling at her, each waiting for the other to take the lead.

Realizing it was up to her, Liza began. "Hello, ma'am, we're here to see how you like your room. Can we talk to you about the service? Is everything to your liking?"

"That's sweet," the woman said. "Everything is delightful." She went to close the door.

"Can we come in?" Liza asked quickly.

"Well . . . I suppose . . ." the woman hesitated.

"We have to check a few things to make sure they're okay," Sam jumped in. "It will only take a moment."

"Certainly, come in." The woman stood aside and let the girls in.

As soon as she was inside, Liza's eyes darted around the room in search of her tape. She didn't see it.

"What do you want to check?" the woman asked.

"The VCR," Liza blurted out. "Lately, they've been breaking down around here."

"It was working fine last night," said the woman. "I was in bed but my husband stayed up watching something. I didn't hear him complain. In fact, he seemed to be enjoying it."

"He was?" Liza said, not quite knowing how to take this information.

At that moment, a man in his early sixties with red curly hair and a long, pointy nose came out of the bathroom wearing a thick blue terry cloth robe. Liza recognized him immediately as Hank Halliday, the president of Plucky Chicken.

"Hello, Mr. Halliday," Sam greeted him.

He took a pair of black-rimmed glasses from his robe pocket and put them on. He peered at Sam. "Oh, yes, my caddy. How are you, dear?"

"Fine, thanks," she answered. "We're the hospitality team today. We're just checking to see . . ." Sam's voice drifted off. It was clear Mr. Halliday wasn't listening. He was staring intently at Liza.

"It's you!" he cried excitedly. "You're the girl on the tape."

"I can explain," Liza said. "The truth about that tape is it—"

"It's fabulous!" he cut her off. "You're exactly what I've been searching for. I guess you missed the deadline for the big competition back in Philadelphia. I'm surprised you even heard of it way down here in Florida, but you got your audition tape to me anyway. That took moxie. I admire that. And luck is on your side. We had selected our gal but she canceled at the last minute. Said she was afraid to take a plane down here."

Liza looked at Chris and Sam. From the expressions on their faces she could tell they had no more of an idea of what he was talking about than she did.

"You're speechless, I see," he continued. "Well, who wouldn't be? It's not every day that a girl is selected to be Miss Plucky Chicken at a national sales convention."

"Miss Plucky what?" asked Liza.

Hank Halliday chortled. "Did you hear that, Millie?" he said to his wife. "The kid has a sense of humor. She's perfect. Miss Plucky What? That's very funny, dear. As if you didn't know you'd just been selected as Miss Plucky Chicken."

"I think there's been a mistake," Chris began. "That tape was supposed—"

"—to do exactly what it did," Liza cut her off. "If you liked it then I'm very, very happy." Liza wasn't sure why she said that, but something told her she might want to hear more about this Miss Plucky Chicken business before turning it down. "What will I have to do?"

"You'll sing and dance and entertain my salespeople. Of course, I'll pay you two hundred dollars for the day."

"Two hundred dollars!" Liza gasped.

Hank Halliday lowered his voice to a whisper. "I'm not promising anything, but I'm considering changing my commercials. The chicken-buying public may be getting tired of seeing my mug. I may want to feature Miss Plucky Chicken in my next commercial."

"I'll do it!" Liza exclaimed excitedly. A national commercial! Lots of people had been discovered doing commercials. Plus, she'd read that if you spoke more than five lines in a commercial, it paid a lot of money.

Flattered that he'd been so impressed with her talents, Liza decided then and there that Hank Halliday was an extremely nice man with excellent taste. He was obviously a genius at spotting talent. "Which part of the tape convinced you to use me?" she asked, hoping for more compliments.

Hank Halliday let out another of his low, rumbling chortles. "That Grandma Kootchie routine," he laughed. "It was a killer. When I saw that, I knew you'd be perfect."

Liza grinned. "That's one of my favorites, too." *This is great!* she thought. *First I'll be Miss Plucky Chicken on TV commercials. Then I'll go to the daytime soaps and then movies.* . . . She and Hank Halliday stood smiling at one another for a moment. "What do I do next?" she asked finally.

"When can you meet me at the convention room?" he asked.

"Tomorrow at one o'clock when my shift ends," she told him.

"Fabulous," he said. "I'll be there with Susan Jones, who's in charge of Miss Plucky Chicken for us each year. You'll like her. She studied theater in college before she became a regional director with the company."

"I can't wait!" Liza said. "Okay, see you tomorrow," she said, backing out of the room.

67

Out in the hall, the girls looked at one another in disbelief.

"That was pretty weird," Sam commented.

"Yeah," Chris agreed. "You went in there a nobody. And you came out . . ."

". . . Miss Plucky Chicken!" Liza finished happily.

Chapter Ten

"Okay, so being Miss Plucky Chicken isn't going to win me an Oscar. But it's a start," Liza said to her friends the next day as she tossed a beach ball into the pool. Liza was so thrilled about this unexpected opportunity that she'd almost forgotten about Miles Lockhart not getting her video.

A boy of five with shaggy blond hair caught the ball and threw it to a four-year-old boy who wore nose plugs, even though he was only waist deep in shallow water. That boy smacked the ball in the direction of Starshine Collins, who was dressed in a silver one-piece suit with three layers of silver ruffles at the waist. Standing on one of the steps leading into the pool, she crossed her arms and let the ball float in front of her.

"Come on, Starshine," Chris coaxed from the edge of the pool where she sat with her legs dangling in the water. "Be nice and play with the boys."

Starshine crossed her arms stubbornly and shook her head.

"Leave her alone for a couple of minutes," Sam suggested. "When she sees the boys playing without her, she might get bored with being stubborn and join the game."

"I hope so," Chris sighed. "Lately I dread coming to work and taking care of that kid. I can't wait for this stupid movie to be over so Luna Collins will take her little terror home."

The ball bounced onto the pool deck. Liza jumped up and ran to retrieve it. "I wish there was a way I could have gotten my video back from Mr. Halliday so I could give it to Miles Lockhart," she said, throwing the ball back to the kids. "But I didn't have the nerve to ask him for it."

"Don't feel too bad," said Sam, wading into the pool past Starshine, who was sitting on the top step sulking. "You might not have gotten into the movie, anyway. Now at least you have something definite—plus two hundred dollars. That's a lot of money."

"I know." Liza smiled. "And if I get into the commercials, who knows what might happen. I'm so nervous. I'm meeting Mr. Halliday today. He'll tell me what I'm supposed to do."

Chris frowned. "What am I going to do about that kid? I can't just leave her sitting there." She got up and went to Starshine. "What would you like to play?" she asked kindly.

"Sea horse!" shouted Starshine, suddenly filled with

jubilant energy. "You be the sea horse and I'll ride you."

Liza laughed when she saw Chris's face. Playing sea horse was obviously not her idea of a good time. *Poor Chris*, thought Liza. Starshine was a handful and she was wearing Chris out. "I'll be the sea horse," she volunteered generously, climbing into the pool.

"Bless you, my child," Chris said with exaggerated relief.

Liza grinned and climbed into the pool, sitting on the steps in front of Starshine. "Hop on," she said.

Starshine leaped onto her back, knocking Liza forward into the water. "Cool down, kiddo," said Liza, recovering her balance and moving out into the slightly deeper water.

"Faster, sea horse. Faster!" yelled Starshine, squirming wildly on Liza's back. She grabbed Liza's hair and yanked on it as if it were the reins of a horse. "Faster!"

"Hey, stop that!" shouted Liza. "Let go of my hair."

Starshine let go, but unfortunately for Liza, she was close enough to the edge of the pool to grab hold of a Styrofoam kick board. "Bad sea horsie!" Starshine shouted, whacking Liza over the head with the board.

"Oooow!" Liza wailed. Stunned by the blow, Liza stood up, dropping Starshine into the water. The little girl held onto the kick board, and in an instant she was kicking to the middle of the pool.

Liza swam out after her. "Come on, Starshine," she called. Starshine pretended not to hear and kept kicking her way across the pool. Starshine was all the way to the opposite side when Liza pounced on her. "Gotcha!"

The girl immediately began to howl, as though Liza

71

were torturing her. Her arms and legs flailing wildly, she tried to squirm from Liza's grasp.

"Need help?" Sam called.

"No, I've got her," Liza called back. She sat Starshine on the side of the pool and then, still holding the little girl's arm, hoisted herself up. *Made it*, she thought, but at that moment a sharp pain made her cry out. Starshine had sunk her teeth into Liza's arm. "Ouch!" Liza shrieked as the girl slipped through her arms.

Starshine raced toward the diving area, and a sharp whistle pierced the air. "No running in the pool area," the lifeguard shouted.

Liza rolled her eyes. Did the lifeguard think she had told Starshine to run? Walking quickly, she caught up with Starshine, who was already up on the low diving board.

Another sharp whistle sounded. "Get that child off the diving board!" the lifeguard shouted at Liza.

"We're coming," Liza heard Chris call. She turned and saw Chris and Sam approaching her, the little boys in tow. Bruce was right behind them. . . . And so was Eddie.

Oh no, what's he doing here? thought Liza despairingly. *I give up. The last time he saw me I was acting like a demented grandmother. This time I'm running after a juvenile maniac.*

"Come down from there," Bruce called, sounding stern. Starshine stuck her tongue out and moved to the edge of the board.

"You can't let her jump!" Chris shouted. "She can't swim."

"What do you want me to do?" Liza yelled back in a

72

panic. Not waiting for Chris's reply, she approached the back end of the board. "Come to me, sweetheart," she said calmly.

"No, no, no!" Starshine said, stamping on the board.

"I have a special surprise for you," Liza called.

Starshine's blond eyebrows raised with interest. "What?"

"Come here and I'll tell you."

Starshine walked toward Liza, but stopped in the middle of the board. "I want to know the surprise first," she demanded.

"Uh, uh," Liza stalled. She hadn't thought that far ahead yet.

"Think of something," Chris hissed. "Luna Collins just came out of the hotel. She hasn't spotted us yet, but she will."

"I'll go ask for her autograph," Eddie volunteered. "I don't work here, so Parker can't say anything to me." Eddie hurried off to waylay the actress.

"Don't you want the surprise?" Chris called to Starshine.

"I'll take you to my show," Liza added quickly. "That's the surprise."

"Your show?" Starshine asked, intrigued.

"Yes. I'm going to be in a show and I'll bring you to see it," said Liza.

"Promise?"

"Promise," Liza assured her, glancing over at Eddie. Luna Collins stood next to him, dressed in a flowing white caftan. She was signing his arm. "Cross my heart,"

73

she told Starshine. That seemed to convince Starshine. She skipped off the board to Liza.

"Thank goodness," said Sam. "Her mother is walking this way."

The actress smiled when she saw them standing by the diving board. "How's my angel?" Luna Collins asked her daughter.

"I'm going to a show, Mommy!" Starshine shouted. "That girl is taking me to her show. She promised."

"Isn't that wonderful," said Luna, scooping Starshine into her graceful arms. "What show is this?"

"I'm in a show for the Plucky Chicken company," Liza explained, feeling slightly foolish.

"Well, isn't it a small world!" exclaimed Luna Collins. "Just today that funny man who's on the commercials—what's his name?"

"Hank Halliday," Sam told her.

"Yes. That's him. Just today he collared Miles and asked him to do commercial spots for Plucky Chicken."

Liza was shocked. Did that mean she might be in commercials with Miles Lockhart? "Is he going to do them?" she asked.

"He's not sure," the actress told her. "He's going to go to their big opening day convention meeting and see what he thinks of the product. I mean, chicken is sort of a tacky product to endorse, don't you think?"

"Not at all," Liza said emphatically. "I mean, not if the commercials are tasteful."

Luna Collins giggled girlishly. "Tasteful. Chicken commercials. Tasteful. Get it?" Everyone laughed politely.

Liza laughed loudest. "At any rate," Luna continued, "maybe you'll see him at the convention show. How will you mind Starshine if you're in the show?"

"That is a problem," Liza admitted. "Maybe I won't be able to bring her, after all."

A storm gathered in Starshine's blue eyes. Her bottom lip jutted out fretfully.

"I'll watch her," Chris volunteered, and Starshine beamed happily.

"You girls have been so nice to my darling," gushed Luna. "I'll have to find some way to thank you."

"It's our job," said Chris.

"And we feel very close to Starshine," Liza added quickly, not wanting Luna to be put off by Chris's lack of enthusiasm. It wasn't every day she had the chance to befriend a major motion picture star. She didn't want anything to ruin it. "She's a beautiful child," Liza continued. "It's our pleasure to sit for such a lively little girl."

"Well, thank you," the actress replied, not detecting Liza's lack of sincerity. "Say good-bye to the nice boys and girls," she told Starshine sweetly.

"Bye, Starshine," they crooned together as the girl and her mother walked back toward the hotel.

"I don't believe you," Sam scoffed. "'She's a beautiful child,'" she mimicked Liza.

"Well, she is pretty," Liza defended herself.

"Oh, come off it," laughed Chris. "That kid is a monster."

"I know she is," Liza admitted, "but I'm not going to tell her mother I think so. Especially not when she talks to Miles Lockhart every day. Do you realize what this means?"

"It means she talks to Miles Lockhart every day," offered Bruce, perplexed.

"It means I'm going to perform in front of Miles Lockhart. He's going to be at the Plucky Chicken convention!"

"That's right. That'll be better than a video," Chris agreed.

"Liza! Live!" shouted Sam.

"We're going to be dead ducks if we don't get these kids back to their parents," Chris reminded Sam. The two little boys they had been watching were chasing one another in circles off to the side of the pool. Chris and Sam called to them.

"I'll walk back to the lobby with you," said Bruce. "Eddie's probably around there."

"Sure," said Chris, smiling at him with dreamy eyes. "You coming?" she asked Liza.

"Start without me," she replied. "I have to go back and get my towel. I left it at the shallow end."

"Get the beach ball, too," Sam reminded her as she and the others headed up to the hotel.

Liza got her towel and then kneeled at the side of the pool and stretched to fish the ball out of the water. Scooping up the ball, which had floated to the side, she found herself staring at a pair of tanned kneecaps.

"Hi," said Eddie, squatting down beside her. He held out his arm with Luna Collins's autograph scrawled across it. "I'll never wash this arm again," he joked. "Did I stall her long enough?"

"You saved my life," Liza answered. "If that woman had seen her daughter about to dive into the pool, she would have croaked. And I'm sure Chris and I would have been fired."

"Glad I could help," he said.

Liza looked into his blue eyes. She liked him so much. There was something about him besides his good looks, something about the way he carried himself. "I think Bruce is looking for you up at the hotel," she told him, feeling suddenly shy.

"I know. I saw him. He told me you were down here."

He'd come down here to see her! That was an excellent sign. "So, what do you think of the hotel?" she asked, trying to make some conversation.

"I can see why they'd film a movie here," he said as they began walking toward the back entrance. "It looks like a movie set."

"Maybe that's why I like working here so much," she said. *Stay calm*, Liza told herself, but she could feel her heart racing. He'd come down to see her! Suddenly she felt herself stumble forward. She'd tripped over a kick board which lay on the side of the pool. Without thinking, she grabbed his arm to keep from falling.

"Whoa," he laughed, holding onto her. "Are you okay?"

"That was pretty klutzy of me. Sorry."

"They shouldn't leave these things lying around," he said, picking up the Styrofoam board and winging it into the empty pool. "I'll have to complain to my good friend Bruce, the pool boy. I have connections in this hotel, you know."

Liza laughed, and they continued to walk toward the hotel. "You know what you said about liking to work here because it's like a movie set?" Eddie said. "I can see you as a movie star."

Liza stopped. "You can?" she asked, pleased by the compliment. "I hope so, because that's what I'd like to be more than anything else in the world."

"You'll make it, I bet," he said. "You're, you know, pretty and you have a good personality."

"No I don't. Well, maybe. I don't know," Liza fumbled, embarrassed but charmed by his words.

"Sure you do. And I know you have talent."

"How do you know?" she asked doubtfully.

"I saw Grandma Kootchie, didn't I?" he answered, his eyes sparkling mischievously.

Liza covered her eyes with her hand. "Don't remind me. That was mortifying."

"It was funny. I liked it," he told her. "I've been in some plays, too."

"You have?" Liza asked, impressed.

"Yeah. We moved here last year, but before that I was in all the plays in my school in Miami."

"Wow! I guess we have a lot in common," said Liza.

"I thought so," he agreed, "the first time I met you."

"I thought so, too," Liza admitted. There was an uncomfortable pause in the conversation. They walked together without talking for a moment. Liza's hand accidently brushed against the side of his. "Um, sorry," she said.

"It's okay," he said, with an embarrassed smile. "I

78

didn't really come to see Bruce today. I came to see if you'd be here. Would you like to go water-skiing with me and some of my friends this Saturday?"

Liza's heart skipped a beat. What a perfect day this was turning into! He liked her and he was asking her out! So what if she didn't know how to water-ski? She'd worry about that later.

She tried to calm herself down. She'd have to be cool.

"Sure," she answered. "What time?"

Chapter Eleven

Liza turned away from her full-length mirror and looked over her shoulder at her reflection. Her red-and-pink floral print, one-piece suit would be perfect for water-skiing.

Facing front, she flipped her long French braid to the right and then to the left. She'd spent a half-hour getting it just right, but now she impulsively tore out the elastic at the bottom and undid it, letting her wavy hair fall freely to her elbows. She bent over, letting her hair fall forward and then flung it back quickly so that it was spread around her shoulders.

"I hope you like the way I look, Eddie," she whispered to the air. "I hope you like everything about me today." She knew he was already interested, but today they would really get to know one another.

Boys had liked Liza before, and she'd been flattered. But no boy had ever gotten to her like Eddie had. No boy had ever made her feel as if she was all arms and legs, as if she couldn't think of a single clever thing to say. It had to be love.

Stepping into a light blue cotton jumpsuit, she adjusted the shoulders, zipped up the front and rolled up the clam-digger-length pants. A pair of straw huarache sandals and some coral lipstick and mascara made the outfit complete. She wished Eddie would arrive right away.

Things are going so great, she thought. During their meeting yesterday, Hank Halliday had introduced her to Susan Jones, the director of the show, who seemed nice. She'd given Liza several songs to learn by their first rehearsal on Monday. The show was going to be next Saturday. It was a little rushed, but Liza didn't mind.

Hank Halliday had explained to her that she would do an opening act and then he would speak to his sales force about upping sales in the coming year. Miles Lockhart would present the Salesperson of the Year award and then she'd return to do a closing number. He seemed to have complete confidence in her. He'd even paid her already. Mrs. Chan had cashed the check for her that very day.

"Liza," her mother called. "Your friend is here."

Thank goodness. She checked herself in the mirror one last time and then hurried through the kitchen but stopped before the living room entrance. It wouldn't do to come charging into the room. "One, two, three," she whispered slowly, to compose herself. Then, as gracefully as she could, she walked in to greet Eddie.

Eddie stood just a step inside the front hall. He wore white shorts and a long yellow cotton shirt. Her mother

81

was sitting on the couch, a magazine open on her lap, talking to him. The twins were sprawled on the floor playing Monopoly. But they looked up to stare at Eddie. That alone was mortifying. Liza hoped no one had said anything too stupid or embarrassing to him.

"Hi," she said. "I guess you've already met my family."

He nodded and smiled. "Ready to go?"

"You be careful on those water-skis," her mother instructed. "I don't want you coming back with any broken bones."

"That's my mother the nurse," said Liza, smiling. "Always worried about my health."

"She's worried because you're a klutz," Hal piped up.

Liza glared at him. "That's not true," said Mrs. Velez.

"Bye!" said Liza, anxious to leave. She took Eddie by the arm and led him to the front door.

"Nice to meet you all," he said politely as they left.

Outside, an old white convertible waited for them. Two boys were in the front seat and two girls were in the back. Liza didn't recognize the boy behind the wheel, but she knew the rest were sophomores at Bonita High. Panic seized her. *They're going to think I'm a stupid little junior-high twerp*, she thought frantically. *They're not even going to speak to me!*

But there was no escaping now. She smiled and approached the car. "The geeks in the front seat are Phil—he's driving—and Allen," Eddie introduced her. "And the ladies in the back are Kelly and Alice."

"Hi, everybody," Liza said, climbing into the back seat. To her relief, they greeted her with friendly smiles.

82

Eddie survived my family, and his friends don't seem to hate me, she thought as the car pulled away from the curb. *Now on to water-skiing—the next possible disaster.*

They drove several miles out of town to Tyler Lake, where Phil's family had a vacation home. Liza sat on the long wooden dock and watched as Phil and Allen pulled up in a small speedboat.

The boys went first. Liza couldn't believe how good Eddie was. He skied on one ski, holding the rope with one hand as he jumped the broad wake created by the fast boat. Although he was clearly the best, all of his friends were confident on the skis.

Eddie joined Phil in the boat so Allen could ski. Then Phil and Allen traded places at the wheel. Liza felt herself growing more and more nervous as her turn neared. Alice went next. She wasn't a great skier, but she got right up and didn't fall. *I'm going to look like such a jerk,* Liza fretted.

"Want to go next?" Kelly asked Liza, as they watched the boat circle around to meet them near the dock.

"No, you go," Liza said with a nervous smile. "I'll wait."

Kelly took her turn, then let go of the line. Sinking gracefully down into the water, she swam the skis back to the dock and climbed out. "Want to start from the water or the dock?" she asked Liza.

"Ummmmm," Liza stalled. Kelly had let her legs dangle from the dock and let the boat pull her along, but Alice had started in the water. That looked slightly easier. "The water," she replied.

Taking a deep breath, Liza buckled on her orange life jacket and jumped into the water. Kelly threw the skis down to her. As Liza struggled with one ski, the other one floated out of her reach. Eddie stood at the back of the boat and watched Liza flounder after the floating ski, with a ski already on one foot.

To her relief, Eddie took an oar from the boat and scooted the loose ski back her way. "Thanks," she called up to him.

Liza continued to struggle with the ski. Suddenly there was a splash and Eddie was quickly beside her. "Need a hand?" he asked.

"Eddie," Liza whispered as he helped her put on the second ski. "There's something I think I should tell you."

"What's that?" he asked, lining up the tips of the skis in front of her.

"I've never done this before."

His eyes lit up with laughter. Liza thought he was going to tease her and say it was pretty obvious that she didn't know what she was doing—but he didn't. "It's easy," he said instead. "You'll get the hang of it after a few flops. Just sit back and let the boat pull you up."

"I'll try," she said, smiling nervously.

Eddie climbed back onto the boat and threw her the tow line. The first three times, she belly-flopped forward into the water. "You're trying to pull yourself up," he called from the back of the boat. "Let the boat do the work."

Liza lined her skis up again. *This is so mortifying*, she thought miserably. Looking around at Eddie's friends, she saw that they were all watching her, waiting to see if she'd make it up. Don't watch, she wanted to tell them. She, who'd never had stage fright, was suddenly in knots of self-consciousness.

When Phil revved the engine, she clutched the tow line and felt the tug of the boat as it carried her to a standing position. She held her breath with excitement as she bumped along behind the boat.

"Get out of the wake," Phil called over his shoulder as he steered. He waved her to go to the left. Instinctively she threw her weight left and it carried her into the smoother water.

Liza was thrilled as the wind whipped her hair and the water tingled as it sprayed her face.

Eddie stood at the back of the boat and gave her a thumbs-up. Liza tried to smile back, but it broke her concentration, throwing her off-balance. For a few minutes her bottom was skimming the surface of the water as she struggled to right herself, then she went over, her legs flying in the air.

The boat slowed down and circled back for her. "You did great," Eddie called when she surfaced.

"That was so much fun," she cried, flipping her wet hair from her eyes. "I loved it."

He fished out the ski which had floated free when she fell, and then helped her up into the boat. "Phil's going to take us back for some lunch now, okay?" he said, handing her a towel.

"Great," Liza said.

Back at the house, Phil's parents were having a

barbecue. "This house is closed up for most of the year," Eddie explained as he put a piece of barbecued chicken on her plate. "But they vacation here for a week or two, or come down for long weekends. I've known Phil since we were kids."

"Wow," Liza murmured, looking at the large, low house with its wraparound screened-in porch. "Imagine being able to afford a house this nice just for vacations." Suddenly she felt awkward. Maybe all these people had enough money to afford that. Would Eddie think less of her because she didn't?

But she didn't have to worry. Eddie put her right at ease. "I can't imagine it, but maybe someday when you're a big star this will seem like nothing to you."

They took their plates and sat beneath a tall palm tree. Liza hadn't told him about being Miss Plucky Chicken, afraid he'd think it was stupid. Now, though, she felt so comfortable with him that she told him the whole story.

He leaned back on his elbows and laughed when she told him about pretending to be the hospitality committee. "And so, anyway, that's how I got the part," she concluded. "It wasn't the part I had in mind, but it's a part."

"You may get the part you want when Miles Lockhart shows up at the convention," he said.

"Keep your fingers crossed," she agreed.

He laid back on the grass and stretched his arms behind his head. Liza couldn't help but notice the muscles that rippled along his upper arms. "You should call the local newspapers," he suggested.

Liza plucked a piece of grass. "They wouldn't be interested."

"Sure they would. 'Local Talent Appears at National Convention.' Hey, no offense, but in Bonita Beach anything is news. And Miles Lockhart is going to be there."

"That's true," Liza agreed. "It would be nice to have the clipping. Maybe I could send it to some director someday when I'm looking for work."

Eddie stood up. "Let's go call now," he said, extending his hand to her.

She let him pull her up. "Now?"

"Yeah, we'll ask Phil's parents if we can use the phone. They're only local calls."

They ran up to the house, and Eddie got permission to use the phone. They went inside to a cool, air-conditioned living room furnished with casual, beachy furniture. The slim, yellow Bonita Beach directory was near the phone. Liza sat beside Eddie on the couch as he flipped through it.

"We'll start with the *Bonita Beach Star*," he said, dialing the phone number.

Liza smiled and bit her lip excitedly as he waited for someone to answer. "Hello," he said in a confident tone of voice. "I'm the press agent for the Palm Pavilion Hotel calling to inform your paper that we will be hosting a very important sales convention on the . . ." He looked at her with questioning eyes.

"Next Saturday," she whispered.

"Next Saturday. Miles Lockhart will be there and we'll be introducing a bright new talent. A local girl, Ms.

87

Liza Velez. Yes, that's with a Z in the middle of Liza and one at the end of Velez. We look forward to seeing your reporter there," he said, hanging up the phone.

"'A bright new talent?'" Liza said, laughing. "I don't believe you're doing this!"

Eddie smiled and went back to the directory. He called the local *Shopper*, the weekly *Entertainment Guide*, and even the *Bonita Beach Clarion*, which was a small paper that specialized in covering the arts.

"Yes, Miss Velez is a theater artist you won't want to miss," he told the *Clarion* editor. "Her work is very deep. Very deep indeed. Fine. We'll see you there."

"The *Clarion* guy is going to have a fit," said Liza. "This is a chicken convention!"

"Did you ever see that paper?" Eddie asked scornfully. "It's a mess. They'll be happy to have a real story about something other than the flight of the flamingo, or whatever."

Eddie reached under the end table and pulled out a fat white directory. "Now for the big gun," he announced.

"Who are you calling?" Liza asked.

"Wait and see," he said. With a twinkle of mischief in his eyes, he dialed a number and asked for the entertainment editor's extension. After a moment, he said, "Hello," and began to describe Liza's upcoming performance at the convention. "Fine, then we can count on you to be there." He hung up the receiver.

"Who was that? Tell me," pleaded Liza.

"The entertainment editor of the *Downstate Monitor*."

"No. You're joking!" gasped Liza. The *Downstate*

Monitor was the most widely read paper in the whole southern half of the state.

"It's no joke. He's coming," said Eddie proudly. "Hey, stick with me, kid," he added in a comical voice. "I'll make you a star."

"Will you be there?" she asked.

"I wouldn't miss it for anything."

"That's so great, Eddie," Liza cried, filled with happiness. Without thinking, she threw her arms around him and hugged him. Suddenly, she realized what she had done and pulled back.

Eddie kept hold of her though. Their eyes met and he gave her a warm smile. And then he kissed her.

Chapter Twelve

"You have to calm down," said Sam to Liza. "You're so wound up you're going to spin right off the planet." Sam knew Liza had a lot of energy but she had never seen her like this before.

It was Monday afternoon and they were sitting in the front row of the hotel's convention center auditorium. They had finished their baby-sitting shift and now Liza was waiting for Susan Jones to arrive so they could go over her act. She'd invited Chris and Sam to watch.

"I'm so excited about this show," said Liza. "Thanks to Eddie—who is just the most wonderful guy in the whole world—five newspapers are coming. And, of course, Miles Lockhart is going to be there. I even invited old Mr. Schwartz."

"And Starshine Collins will be there," groaned Chris.

"Forget about her," said Liza. "My whole life could change next Saturday. The papers will write about me. Miles Lockhart will let me be in his movie. And Eddie will fall even more madly in love with me once I'm in the spotlight. This will be the moment my whole life has been leading up to."

"Don't you think you're over-dramatizing a bit?" said Sam.

"There's excited and then there's demented," Chris stated drily. "You are dangerously close to turning into a maniac."

"Oh, you two are spoilsports," Liza brushed them off. "Don't you see? This is my time to shine! I mean, look at this great room I'm going to be performing in."

"This place reminds me of the school auditorium," Sam said.

"It's much nicer," Liza insisted. The room was painted a pale rose color that matched the seats. The stage was rather small, and a narrow runway extended from its center. Liza hopped up onto the runway. "Here I am, Miss America," she sang playfully, pretending to hold a bunch of roses in the crook of her elbow.

Chris hopped up beside her, holding an imaginary microphone. "I have a question for you, Miss Bonita Beach," she said, mimicking the formal tones of a pageant host.

"Just call me Bonita," Liza joked in a high voice. "All my friends do."

"Okay, Chiquita," said Chris.

Liza shoved her lightly. "I said Bonita, not Chiquita."

"Excuse me, Miss Beach. Anyway, what is the most important thing about being Miss America?"

Liza batted her eyes and pouted. "I guess what's most

91

important to me is that I get to blow a big kiss to all my friends over live TV." She giggled and laid a loud slurpy kiss on the palm of her hand, then waved her arm over her head.

Loud applause from the doorway made them stop. "Very funny," chuckled a tall woman with short, curly brown hair. "I can see why Mr. Halliday picked you." Susan Jones walked toward them.

Liza introduced her to Chris and Sam, and then they began working on the show. To begin with, Liza would sing the welcome song from the play *Cabaret*, but instead of singing, "Welcome to The Cabaret," she would sing, "Welcome to Plucky Chicken."

"You have to remember that this is really a warm-up to the big sales presentation," said Susan. "Your job is to make everyone feel good about the Plucky Chicken company, so that when Mr. Halliday gets up there and demands that they get his chickens into twice as many supermarkets next year, they'll be inspired. You're very important to the success of this sales meeting."

"I didn't realize what a big responsibility this was," said Liza. "You can count on me."

Next, Susan asked Liza to rehearse the Plucky Chicken song. She slipped a tape of the music into a cassette player and turned it on. Liza sang the song, which she'd memorized over the weekend.

"She sounds good," Sam whispered to Chris.

"Yeah," Chris agreed. "Real good. Considering it's such a dumb song. These people sure get revved up over chickens."

"I hope this works out for her," said Sam. "I'd hate for her to be disappointed. Her hopes are so high. Maybe they're too high."

"I know what you mean," said Chris. "But maybe we're just being pessimists. What could possibly go wrong?"

"Right," Sam said, settling down in a chair. It's just that she didn't trust things that seemed so perfect. She wasn't sure why. Maybe that was her way of protecting herself against disappointment. And now, in her own way, she was trying to protect Liza from being disappointed.

Susan worked with Liza on some gestures and a few quick dance steps to liven up the performance. Then they went over a dance routine set to a lively barnyard song. Next, they practiced a welcoming speech Susan had written. The speech talked about how sales were up and how the salespeople were all to be commended for a fine year's work. "And some of you may be thinking, this is some crummy reward, having to go to the south of Florida in the middle of summer," Liza read from the typewritten sheet Susan had handed her. "But some cool bonus cash in your next pay envelopes may help you beat the heat. If that doesn't cool you off, just think about how I feel in this costume!"

Liza looked up from the sheet. "I'm going to get a costume?"

"Yes," Susan answered. "Didn't Mr. Halliday tell you?"

"No. He never mentioned—"

At that moment Hank Halliday burst through the

door. "How's Miss Plucky Chicken today?" he shouted from the back of the room.

"I'm fine," Liza called back. "Mr. Halliday, is there some kind of special costume that I'm supposed to—"

"Have it right here," he said, holding up a package wrapped in brown paper. "Just arrived by parcel post from my Philadelphia office. The gals back there were fluffing it up."

Liza peered at the package with great interest, but Sam couldn't help noticing Susan's look of concern. "I wonder what this costume looks like," she said to Chris.

Chris shrugged. "It's probably some kind of farm girl outfit."

Liza stood at the end of the runway as Hank Halliday broke the twine and pulled off the paper. "Here she is," he said proudly, lifting up what looked like a yellow boa.

From where she was sitting, Sam couldn't quite see the costume. What she did see was Liza's expression change from one of curiosity to complete horror. "But . . . but . . . Mr. Halliday," she stammered. "That costume. It's . . . it's a chicken costume!"

"Of course it is," Hank Halliday answered enthusiastically. "But it's not any chicken, it's Miss Plucky Chicken. See the bow in her hair?" He held up a large, beaked head full of wispy yellow feathers. Two large white eyes had holes cut in them, and the chicken had a large red bow on the top of her head.

"And look at this cute checked skirt that goes around the waist," he added, pulling out a ruffled piece of material.

"That skirt's much too big for me," Liza objected.

"It won't be once you put this on." He began blowing up what looked like an oversized yellow life jacket. "This will fill out the costume," he said between puffs. "We couldn't have Miss Plucky Chicken be scrawny now, could we? Wouldn't exactly be the image we're going for. Don't forget, Plucky Chickens are plump and juicy."

He handed the inflated vest to Liza. She took it, holding it away from herself as if it were diseased. Hank Halliday didn't seem to notice. "This is the best part," he said, plunking two oversized orange chicken feet down on the runway. "They take a little getting used to, but you'll be able to manage them."

Liza looked down at the giant rubber feet standing in front of her and then gazed helplessly at Sam and Chris. Sam got up and walked to the runway with Chris right behind her and picked up a chicken foot. The claws were mounted over a black sneakerlike high-top shoe. She opened her mouth but no words came out. What was there to say? Disaster had struck, after all.

Hank Halliday turned to Susan Jones. "Come with me a second. I want you to look at a chart I've drawn up for the big presentation."

Susan apologized to Liza and followed her boss out of the room. The girls stared at one another in disbelief.

"Cute costume," said Chris, finally.

Liza flung the other chicken foot at her. "This can't be happening," she said. "I know that I'm really home in bed having a terrible nightmare and soon I'll wake up. That's right, isn't it?"

"If it is, then the three of us are having the same nightmare," Sam told her reluctantly.

"What am I going to do?" Liza moaned. "The newspapers! Miles Lockhart! Eddie! They're all coming! Coming to see me dancing around in a chicken costume! It's too mortifying. I can't do it."

"You could give back the money," Chris suggested.

Liza's face went pale. "No I can't. I already spent it."

"So fast?" Sam questioned her.

"Sunday I bought a new VCR for my family," she said. "Ours was broken."

"Can you return it?" asked Chris.

Liza shook her head. "I bought it at a store that allows only exchanges or store credit, but no refunds." Liza turned the chicken shoe over and over in her hand. "Looks like I'm stuck, huh?"

Chris and Sam nodded.

Liza stuck the end of the chicken foot into her mouth—and screamed.

Chapter Thirteen

Early that evening, Liza came in the front door of her house and headed straight to her room. The twins were lying on the floor watching a movie on the new VCR.

"This VCR is great," Jimmy said to her. "The picture isn't all fuzzy like with the other one."

Liza gazed for a moment at the VCR which she had so impulsively and happily bought the day before. Why had she been so stupid? If she still had the money, she could give it back and that would be that.

She heard her mother talking on the phone in the kitchen. Could she ask her for a two-hundred-dollar loan? Maybe. She'd pay her back with her baby-sitting money.

Liza stood in the living room just outside the kitchen door. She wanted to listen to her mother's conversation to gauge her mood.

"No, you don't have to worry about it anymore, Rick," her mother said. She was talking to Liza's father.

Doesn't sound too promising, thought Liza, *although she seems kind of happy.*

"Yes, Liza bought it with her own money," her mother continued proudly. "I know. . . . Can you believe it? Our little girl is growing up. . . . I'm proud of her, too. I get mad at her sometimes, but she is a sweet girl. And you know, I thank heaven she bought it. The twins were driving me nuts without it, but I simply couldn't afford to replace the old one right now. The transmission on the car is shot, and I can't decide whether to try to fix it or get another used car. Either way it's going to cost a fortune. . . . No, that was not a hint. . . . Did I ask you for car money? . . . All right then, drop it. . . ."

Liza drifted away from the door. No way. She couldn't ask for a loan after hearing that conversation. She squared her shoulders and walked through the kitchen, hoping to get to her bedroom without stopping.

"Here she is now," her mother said. "Want to say hi to Daddy?"

She wasn't in the mood, but how could she say no? Liza took the receiver from her mother. "Hi, Dad."

"Your mother told me about your gift to the family. I'm very proud of you."

"Thanks," she replied glumly.

"And she says you're in a show this Saturday. Terrific. I want to come. When and where is it?"

"No!" she nearly shouted. "No. You don't want to come."

"Of course I do. Don't I always come to your—"

"Uhhh. Not this one. No—ummm—no outsiders are

98

allowed. It's strictly for salespeople. Sorry, but that's the rule."

"You're sure?" he pressed, disappointed.

"Positive. Absolutely positive. Mr. Halliday was very firm about that."

"All right, then. But I'll be imagining you up there on that stage knocking them dead."

"Thanks, Dad." Somehow Liza doubted he'd be picturing her hopping around in a chicken costume. "Believe me, you're not missing anything," she added. "I have to go now, Dad."

"Okay, good luck. Put your mother back on, please. I love you."

Liza handed her mother the phone and went to her room. After Hank Halliday had left the rehearsal, Susan returned and apologized about the costume. She'd assumed Liza knew about it. Liza had begged her to talk Mr. Halliday out of it, but Susan said it was no use. Mr. Halliday was not a man known to change his mind, and Miss Plucky Chicken had been appearing at every convention for the last ten years. Mr. Halliday was almost superstitious about her. The chicken costume was like a good luck charm to him, Susan had told Liza.

"Why can't he carry a fake rabbit's foot like everybody else?" Liza mumbled, lying face down on her bed. She'd thought it through until her head ached. It was becoming painfully clear that there was simply no way out of this completely humiliating situation. "How do you get yourself into these messes, Liza?" she muttered, pulling her pillow over her face.

She was lying like that, just wishing the world would go away, when there was a knock on her door. "Eddie is here to see you," called her mother.

"I'll be there in a second." Liza jumped up, pulled off her Palm Pavilion staff polo shirt, and changed into a canary yellow cotton tank top. Depressed as she was, she wanted to look her best for Eddie.

She found him sitting on the couch in the living room, watching the movie with the twins. "Is this the new VCR?" he asked when he saw her.

"That's it," she answered flatly. She saw him stiffen, and realized he thought her attitude had something to do with him. "Don't mind me," she told him. "It's hot and I had a hard day at work."

Somehow she just couldn't bear to tell him about the chicken costume. She knew he had a good sense of humor, but this was too much. If Grandma Kootchie hadn't completely destroyed the air of mystery and feminine allure she was trying to create, this certainly would. How could he ever take her seriously after this?

"You sure nothing else is wrong?" he asked.

"I'm sure," she said. "Come on out to the back porch." They went out onto the open porch. It was a bright night; the moon outlined everything in silver, and a warm breeze blew. Two brown moths bumped continually into the globe lamp that hung from the porch ceiling.

"I came over to tell you that I called one more paper today. My boss at Flamingo Pizza subscribes to one called *Local Business*. It's put out for shop owners to keep them informed of local business affairs. They run short articles, so I called them and they said they'd send somebody to the show."

"That's great," Liza said listlessly.

"You don't sound too thrilled."

"I don't know, Eddie," she said, leaning forward. "I'm afraid the show won't be as good as I thought it would be. I'm afraid it will be a bomb. Maybe you shouldn't even come."

His eyes scanned her face as though they were looking for clues to her real feelings. "If you don't want me—"

"It's not that. I just think you'd be bored," she said.

"You couldn't bore me."

"No, really. I'd rather you didn't come," she insisted.

"The show doesn't have to be perfect. I don't care if—"

"I want to do this alone, okay?" she said.

He stood and moved toward the porch steps. "Look, if that's the way you feel, I understand," he said with a hint of anger in his voice.

"Eddie, don't be mad," she pleaded.

"I'm not mad. I said I understand."

"Eddie!" she cried.

"I have to go," he said quickly. "See ya." With that, he turned and walked down the steps, disappearing down the dark driveway.

Chapter Fourteen

"Stop squirming, Starshine," Chris scolded. She was holding Starshine's hand, and Starshine was doing her best to wriggle out of Chris's grasp. Chris sighed. She couldn't believe it was Saturday and she was still stuck with this brat. It was the afternoon of the Plucky Chicken show. She, Sam and Liza were standing in front of the convention room door.

"Here goes nothing," said Liza, her yellow chicken costume in a large shopping bag under her arm. She was resigned to her fate. Yesterday she'd run through the routine with Susan. Wearing the horrible costume, she felt like a fool. She knew her performance wasn't very good, either. It was hard to give it her all when she was depressed and roasting. It felt like a hundred degrees inside that costume.

"I coming with you," cried Starshine, latching on to the bottom of Liza's shirt. "I want be in show, too."

"You don't want to be in *this* show," Liza assured her.

She turned to Sam, who had volunteered to be an usher. "Thanks for doing this," Liza told her. The plan was for Sam to look for members of the press and direct them away from the convention room. "At least it will help not to have press coverage of my most embarrassing moment," she said, opening the door to go inside.

"What should I do if I see Eddie?" Sam asked.

"You won't see him," Liza said. "He's mad at me."

"Why?" asked Chris.

"I told him not to come to the show."

"Did you explain why?" Sam asked. Liza shook her head. "Liza!" Sam cried. "Why not?"

"Sorry, Eddie," Liza said in a squeaky voice. "I'd rather you didn't see me dancing in a chicken costume." She rolled her dark eyes. "How could I say that?"

"I don't know," Sam admitted, "but you should have told him something."

"I guess," said Liza. "I can't think about that now. It's showtime." She stepped inside the convention auditorium, letting the door swing shut behind her.

Chris looked at Sam and then nodded in the direction of a short, fat man coming toward them with a large camera around his neck.

"*Bonita Star*," he announced proudly to the girls. "Is this the Plucky Chicken Show?"

"Ummm, well, yes and no," Sam hesitated. "Uh, the press will receive a special briefing in the . . . uh . . . Guacamole Room in the . . . the . . . Avocado Tower."

"Where do I find that?" he asked, looking perplexed.

Sam looked at Chris for help. "Uh, down that hall," Chris said, pointing behind her, "down the stairs and out the back door. Follow the path until you come to an aqua door. Wait there. Someone will let you in."

"Okay. Thanks," he said, bustling down the hall.

"You sent him to the spa," Sam said, trying not to laugh.

"Well where did you expect me to direct him? The Guacamole Room. I don't believe you! The Avocado Tower. How did you think those names up?"

"I don't know. They just came to me," said Sam. "Well, it worked, anyway. Let's stick to that story."

"It's not going to take them that long to figure out they're in the wrong place," Chris pointed out.

"We could tell them the show has already started, and no one is admitted until after the first act," Sam suggested.

"There is only one act," said Chris.

"Exactly," said Sam.

Chris grinned at Sam. "You act like such a law-abiding citizen, but you have a very devious mind."

"Thank you," said Sam. "I think."

"I want to see the chicken show!" wailed Starshine, drawing their attention back to her.

"How can such a cute kid be such a pain?" Chris asked Sam. The little girl did look especially sweet today. Her blond curls were tied up in a red ribbon on top of her head. She wore a blue and white polka-dotted dress that flared into a short ruffled skirt, and a pair of red leather sandals.

"Maybe you should take her inside," suggested Sam.

"No, I'll wait out here with you until the last minute," said Chris. The thought of keeping Starshine quiet as they waited didn't appeal to her. At least there was some action out in the hall to distract her. "Can you count, Starshine?" Chris asked her.

Starshine nodded proudly.

"Good, then you count all the people who go through that door and tell me how many are inside. All right?"

"Okay," Starshine agreed eagerly. "One, two, three, five, six, nine, one . . ."

Around two o'clock, people began to stream into the auditorium. Chris found it easy to tell the salespeople from the press. The salespeople were dressed in summer suits. A lot of them were peeling or sunburned, obviously not used to the hot summer sun of southern Florida. They all seemed to know where the presentation show was and headed straight into the convention auditorium.

The members of the press, on the other hand, were dressed more casually. They were evenly and lightly tanned. Some had cameras or were accompanied by a photographer. And they all looked lost.

They were soon even more lost as Chris and Sam directed them to the spa at the far end of the Palm Pavilion's beach. "Let's see, we sent six reporters and two photographers that way," said Sam. "That should be everyone we were supposed to get rid of."

"Yeah, but what do we do about him?" asked Chris. Eddie was coming toward them down the hall. "I thought Liza told him not to come. She's going to be mortified."

Sam shrugged. "I don't know what we can do. He knows where he's going. We can't stop him."

"Hi, Eddie," said Chris, noticing that he had a small bouquet of yellow rosebuds in his hand.

"Hi," he said. He looked uncomfortable for a moment. "Did Liza tell you that we had a fight?"

"She mentioned it," said Chris. "But she's just uptight about this show. She'll be back to her normal self when it's over."

"I know," he said. "I acted like a jerk. I should have realized she was nervous. So that's why—"

"There's ten one hundred people," Starshine announced. "Now I want to see the show."

"One second, Starshine," said Chris. "Eddie, I'm not sure you should go in there. Ummm, they only want salespeople and—"

Chris's words were cut short by a sharp poke from Sam. She followed Sam's gaze up the hall toward the lobby. Miles Lockhart was coming toward them, with a mob of reporters—some with TV cameras and microphones hanging from rods—trailing after him.

"Is it true, Miles, that you are about to sign a multimillion-dollar advertising contract with Plucky Chicken?" Chris heard a reporter ask.

Miles shot her his famous, disarming grin. "That's what I'm here to decide," he said.

"We hear you're going to present the Plucky Chicken Salesperson of the Year plaque at this event," said another reporter.

"That is correct. Since I'm down here making my soon-to-air TV movie *Alien Wind*, I figured it never hurts to help out a potential sponsor," he joked.

"That's a fabulous photo opportunity, Miles," said a photographer. "Can we come in and snap a few shots?"

"Hey, it's free advertising for Plucky Chicken," he told them. "You're all welcome."

"Oh, no," gasped Sam. "Now Liza is going to be on TV. She's going to die."

Just then, the reporters came running up the hall from the opposite direction. "There he is! Miles Lockhart!" one of them shouted. They raced for the door just as Miles opened it. He noticed Starshine as he was about to step into the auditorium. "Hi, sweetheart," he said, also nodding at Sam and Chris.

"I going to the show," she told him.

"I've just been told there will be a little show with this presentation," he said to the reporters with a wink. "I'm sure you'll want to cover it in your story."

The crowd of reporters followed Miles into the auditorium. Chris and Sam looked at one another with forlorn expressions. "Liza will certainly be pleased when she sees the fine job we did keeping the reporters out of the auditorium," said Chris sarcastically. "Now, instead of six, there are only about a zillion of them."

"I guess Miles Lockhart's press agent called all of them," Sam said.

"I don't get this," said Eddie. "What's wrong with the press being here? I mean, isn't that what Liza wanted?"

"It's kind of hard to explain," said Chris weakly.

107

"Something is weird here," he said, pulling open the door. "None of this makes sense. I'm going to see for myself."

"Come on, Starshine," Chris said wearily. "We might as well join the party."

Chapter Fifteen

Liza felt as if her skin was about to melt off her bones as she peered out of the two eyeholes cut in the chicken head. Even though the auditorium was air-conditioned, none of the cool air penetrated the thick, feather-covered rubber of her chicken costume.

She watched from behind the stage curtain as the auditorium filled with salespeople. Then she heard a rising clamor. Leaning out a little farther, she spotted Miles Lockhart—and a crowd of reporters.

She stepped back behind the curtain. How had this happened? How had a sales meeting turned into a media event? Miles Lockhart. That was how.

Liza felt herself growing faint. She pushed up the chicken head to get some air. "You go on in two minutes," said Susan Jones, coming up behind her.

"I don't know if I can," Liza said in a pitiful voice.

Susan clutched Liza's feathery arm. "You have to," she

said, her voice tinged with panic. "I mean, we're counting on you."

"I feel kind of—" Liza began.

"If you don't go, Mr. Halliday will have my head. This presentation is my responsibility. And with all those reporters out there, you just can't—"

Liza could see that Susan was about to lose her cool altogether. "Okay, okay. I'm going," she said.

"Great, great. You'll be great," Susan told her, fluffing the chicken feathers nervously. "Give them another minute to settle down, and then I'll put the tape in the stereo."

Susan scurried off behind the stage. Liza peeked out again and spotted Chris sitting up front near the center of the runway with Starshine at her side. Starshine wasn't sitting, though. She was waving at everyone, as though she were the star of the show. Just behind Chris sat Sam, looking concerned and unhappy. And next to her was—Eddie! *Oh, no!* Liza thought mournfully. *Can this get any worse?*

The crowd quieted down as Miles Lockhart took a seat in the front row next to Hank Halliday. Liza saw the audience looking toward the stage expectantly. This was it.

Susan turned on the tape, and the opening music began. Liza felt as if a brick had formed in the pit of her stomach. "Pssst! Go!" Susan hissed in a stage whisper.

Liza forced herself to put one chicken-clawed foot in front of the other. She stepped out from behind the curtain, and she immediately wobbled off-balance. She staggered back two steps and then recovered.

110

She moved to the center of the stage and began to sing. "Welcome to Plucky Chicken. Welcome." She was in the middle of the first verse when she noticed Hank Halliday desperately mouthing something to her. She flapped her way over toward him. His mouth was moving in wide "o" shapes. Louder. She realized he was mouthing the word louder.

She saw what he meant. People were whispering to one another, not paying attention at all. She tried to sing louder, but her voice cracked into a small squeak. Hot tears stung her eyes and her voice broke again.

Forcing herself to continue, she did a half-hearted strut down the runway. All around her, people were carrying on private conversations. She saw Eddie leaning back in his chair, his arms folded, his brows knit in confusion. Maybe he didn't even know she was in the costume. He was probably waiting for her to come on.

She kicked her clawed foot out as Susan had taught her. "Welcome to Plucky Chicken, to Plucky Chicken, to Plucky Chicken," Liza croaked on feebly.

Below her, she saw Chris struggling with Starshine, pulling on the little girl's dress so she'd sit down. "I want be in show!" she wailed, reaching up toward the runway.

Suddenly, Liza came up with an idea. Still singing, she hopped off the stage in front of Chris and Starshine. "Bring her backstage," she said quickly to Chris.

Liza then tried to get back up on the runway and discovered that getting down had been much easier. The bulky costume made it almost impossible to climb back up. She was stuck on the edge, her chicken feet flailing behind.

Chris shoved her up just as the tape ended. Liza lumbered to her feet. She had to do something. "Welcome!" she shouted. "We'll be right back after a two-minute break."

She ran backstage and ripped off her chicken head. Then she unzipped the chicken suit. That had been a total disaster, but there was no time to feel sorry for herself now.

Chris had run up the side steps with Starshine and quickly ducked behind the curtain. Sam was right behind them. "Are you okay?" Sam asked.

"I will be," said Liza, detaching the chicken wings from the costume and draping them around Starshine's shoulders.

"What are you doing?" Chris asked.

"You want to be in the show, don't you, Starshine?" said Liza. Starshine nodded furiously. "Okay, you can be my little chick. You just dance to the music, okay?"

"I be in show!" Starshine cried.

"Here, wear this," Liza said, plunking the chicken head down over Starshine's shoulders. The head fell almost down to her elbows. "You okay in there?" asked Liza.

"I be in show!" she answered joyfully.

"Give me your brush," Liza told Chris. Chris reached into her purse and handed Liza a brush. Liza quickly ran it through her sweat-drenched, matted hair. She took the rest of the chicken costume and twisted it into a long

112

boa of feathers. Then she threw it over her shoulders. "Lipstick," she commanded. Chris dug in her purse and handed her a tube.

"What's going on?" cried Susan Jones, hurrying up behind them.

"I'm making a little change," Liza told her. "If you hate it, I'll find some way to pay back the money."

"You can't just—" Susan objected.

"Sorry," Liza cut her off. "The show must go on."

Holding Starshine's hand, Liza walked out on stage. Summoning all her nerve, she spoke up loudly. "Welcome to the Plucky Chicken Sales Convention," she said. For the first time the room quieted. "That sad sack of a chicken you just saw was the old Plucky Chicken. My little friend here is the new Plucky Chick. She's bringing in a whole new year of sales. She's peppy and lively and she's gong to be in every store next year. Say hi to the nice folks, Plucky Chick."

Starshine waved with both hands, thrilled to be the center of attention. "Plucky Chick is going to do a little dance for you, while I sing the Plucky Chicken Song."

On cue, the taped music came on. Starshine didn't miss a beat. She twirled and then hopped up and down as Liza belted out the Plucky Chicken song:

"Our chicks are swell. They're all great. They're the plumpest chicks you ever ate! Starting here. Starting now. Every store's carrying Plucky Chickens!"

As she sang, Starshine hopped, kicked and twirled. She had obviously been around theater people all her life and inherited her mother's theatrical flair. There wasn't a shy bone in her body. Liza's eyes went wide with delight as Starshine broke into a tap routine that clearly showed she'd taken lessons.

"Our chickens . . . on your plate . . . they're just nothing short of great. Thighs, breasts, drumsticks too. Honey, Plucky Chickens are the best chicks for me and for you!" As Liza belted out the end of the song, Starshine jumped up and down enthusiastically.

The crowd roared with laughter, applauding wildly. She had them. Liza's heart pounded. They loved her. And Starshine.

"Thank you," she called over the applause. She put her hand on Starshine's shoulder to stop her from bowing. "Now I'd like to say a few words about Plucky Chicken."

Liza gave the speech Susan had written for her, changing it here and there to include the new Plucky Chick. Her natural showmanship—or, as Chris would say, her hamminess—carried her along. Now and then a ripple of laughter erupted in a bewildering spot. She would turn and see Starshine, peeking out under her chicken head and making silly faces at the audience. Liza smiled and didn't stop her. Whatever made the audience happy was fine with her.

When her speech was over, Liza did the farmyard dance with Starshine. She spun the little girl around square-dance style. Again, Starshine was a natural. Getting into the spirit, she even began clucking at the top of her little lungs. The audience was enchanted.

At the end of the dance, Liza lifted the chicken head

from Starshine's shoulders. "This is Little Plucky Chick, Starshine Collins. I'm Liza Velez, and we both hope you have a terrific sales year. Thank you!"

With Starshine bowing madly, Liza held her hand and they backed off the stage. "I be in show!" Starshine shouted.

"You were great!" cried Liza, planting a kiss on her pudgy cheek.

"You were super great!" said Chris to Liza, jumping up and down excitedly.

"The best!" Sam agreed, hugging Liza.

The crowd continued to applaud. "Go on, take another bow," Susan said, gently pushing them back onstage.

Holding hands, Liza and Starshine took another bow. They were about to go off when Miles Lockhart walked on the stage with Hank Halliday.

Liza's mouth dropped open, stunned, as Miles stood between her and Starshine, clapping. Liza smiled at him. *He liked it*, she thought. *He liked my performance!*

There was a staticky rasp of microphone as Hank Halliday began to speak. "A fresh new approach to selling the freshest chickens in town," he announced. "Now we are very honored to have that illustrious star of stage and screen, Miles Lockhart, here to present the Salesperson of the Year Award. I'll have a lot to say afterwards, but for now I'll keep my beak shut and give you everyone's favorite—Miles Lockhart."

Liza moved to leave the stage, but Miles motioned for her and Starshine to stay. "Before I give the award, I want to take a moment to commend our entertainers on

115

a fine job," he said. "I know them. Miss Plucky Chick is the daughter of my dear friend and co-star Luna Collins. I never realized she was as talented as her mom. And I met Miss Velez the other day when she fell into the pool during the filming of *Alien Wind* here at the fabulous Palm Pavilion."

Liza felt herself blush in embarrassment. But it didn't matter. Miles Lockhart had a way with words that made falling into a pool seem like an entertaining, clever thing to have done.

"I see now that Liza has other talents besides splashing my camera crew." The crowd laughed, clearly captivated by the star's charm. "And if she will consent, I'd like to have her play a role in the closing scene of *Alien Wind*, a scene I recently finished rewriting."

Liza covered her gaping mouth with her hand. It was all happening. Everything she'd dreamed of!

"What do you say, Liza?" Miles asked with an irresistible grin.

"Sure, of course. I—I'd love to," she stammered.

The audience applauded again. "Fabulous," he said. "If her mom agrees, I may even have a little part for Miss Plucky Chick, too. Now," he went on earnestly, "let me talk to you about something serious, the Salesperson of the Year Award." Liza saw it was their cue to leave and ran offstage with Starshine.

"You don't have to worry about paying back any money," said Susan Jones, taking the chicken head from Starshine. "What a great idea!"

"I'm glad you liked it," Liza told her. That's all she had

time to say before Sam and Chris nearly crushed her with hugs.

"You're in the movie! You're in the movie!" Chris whispered hoarsely, trying not to make too much commotion.

"Everything has worked out so great!" gasped Liza, patting Starshine, who was hugging her knees.

"It sure has," Sam agreed.

While the Salesperson of the Year was making her acceptance speech, the girls sneaked quietly down the stairs on the opposite side of the stage. They were walking along the far wall when Liza saw Eddie coming toward her.

He held out the yellow roses. "You were really good," he said. "Sorry I was such a jerk yesterday."

Chris, Sam and Starshine kept walking, leaving Liza alone with Eddie. "You weren't a jerk," she said, cradling the roses in her arms. "I just didn't want you to—"

"I know," he said. "You didn't want me to make you nervous. I understand now. Hey, you know, for a second I almost thought that the first awful chicken was you."

"You did?" said Liza. "Oh, well, uh . . ."

"Yeah," he laughed. "I thought maybe that was why you didn't want me to come. I wouldn't have blamed you."

"Oh, yes," she smiled, slipping her arm through his. "I know what you mean. That certainly would have been embarrassing."

117

Chapter Sixteen

"Liza is going to be too excited when she sees this," said Sam, hopping off her bike and showing Chris the morning edition of the *Bonita Beach Star*.

This morning, Liza hadn't ridden to work with them. She'd gotten the day off so that she could appear in *Alien Wind*. The filming had begun at dawn. Since Liza had been up before any of the papers were even delivered, Sam and Chris assumed she hadn't yet seen the full-page write-up of her performance at the Plucky Chicken Convention.

"'Miles Lockhart Picks Local Talent for Role in Upcoming TV Movie,'" Chris read for the tenth time that morning. "This could be a real beginning for Liza. I wonder if she'll still be friends with us when she's famous."

"She'd better be," said Sam, unable to imagine the three of them not being friends. She squinted and looked around the front of the hotel. "Where do you think they're filming today? It's only eight. We have time to show her the paper before we go in."

They walked to the hotel's front entrance and asked Pierre, the front doorman. "Over on the golf course, I do believe I heard them say this morning," he told them.

They thanked him and headed through a row of trees onto the green lawn. "Oh my gosh! Look!" said Chris, pointing to the right.

"Wow!" said Sam. About five yards away from them stood a huge spaceship with many colored lights blinking on and off. "That's awesome," she murmured.

"I sure hope that's the movie set," said Chris.

"Of course it is," said Sam sensibly. "Come on." The girls trudged across the still-dewy, manicured lawn toward the spaceship. As they got nearer they heard the whoosh of a wind machine that was aimed at the spaceship. "I guess that's the alien wind," Sam surmised.

"The star of the movie!" joked Chris. "Maybe we should get its autograph."

They drew closer and spotted Miles Lockhart dressed in casual shorts and a white polo shirt. He was directing Luna Collins, who stood next to the spaceship, dressed in a gorgeous evening gown which was ripped and dirty. A few strands of her long blond hair were prettily out of place and mud was attractively smeared across her forehead.

Chris and Sam stood among the extras, assistants and camera crew who hovered in a ring around the area that had been cleared for the set. "I don't see Liza," said Chris, craning her neck in search of her friend.

"She said she would be filming this morning. She's got to be here somewhere," said Sam.

"Okay, hon," Miles said to Luna as he ran off the set. "Remember, the aliens have captured me, your husband. You can't live without me, so now you're begging them to take you into outer space, too. Give it all you've got."

Luna nodded and stepped up to the spaceship and into the wind. A fog machine created clouds of mist around her feet. A red light shone, giving the fog an eerie glow. A man stood in front of the cameras and held up a small blackboard with the words *Alien Wind* written across it. He held up a ruler which was attached to the top of the board by a side hinge. "*Alien Wind,* scene twenty-five, take three," he announced as he snapped down the ruler.

Chris and Sam watched, fascinated, as a hatch opened in the spaceship. Five creatures in flowing, gauzy white robes emerged. Their faces were almost featureless, with only wide, soulful eyes and small thin lips.

Luna Collins fell to her knees in the fog. "Please!" she begged dramatically. "Take me with you. I must see Lance again."

The aliens looked at one another as if communicating silently. They came down and surrounded the actress. "I beg you," Luna sobbed.

One of the aliens stepped into the circle. It nodded its head and said, "Ye-e-e–sssssss," in a high squeaky voice.

Chris and Sam looked at one another, shocked. "Do you think?" asked Chris.

"It sounded a little like Grandma Kootchie to me," observed Sam.

Then all the aliens bowed as a very small alien came down the hatch. This one looked the same as the others, except that it wore an elaborate headdress of colored tubes. The tiny creature looked at Luna, squeaked a few times, then turned and went back into the ship.

The alien who had said yes took Luna by the hand and walked her to the ship. The four other aliens went in first, followed by Luna, and then the fifth alien went in and closed the hatch.

"Cut, print! Perfect!" yelled Miles Lockhart.

The wind stopped abruptly and the fog drifted away. The hatch opened and out scrambled Luna Collins, the five aliens and their pint-sized leader.

Chris and Sam watched as one alien pulled off her white rubber mask and a long braid tumbled down. "It *is* her!" cried Chris.

They ran over and hugged Liza. "How was I?" she asked. "Scary?"

"Totally," Chris said.

"Hey, look who's the leader of the pack!" said Sam, pointing at the tiny alien. Luna Collins peeled the little creature's mask off Starshine's face. The girl caught sight of Sam, Chris and Liza and waved.

"I be in show!" she cried happily.

Sam and Chris showed Liza the newspaper. She read it, her eyes glowing with pride. She looked down at her white robe and chuckled. "It's a start, anyway," she said.

"It's a movie!" said Sam.

"This will make great trivia, too," noted Chris. "What was Liza Velez's very first movie? No one would guess this."

"No one but my two very best friends," Liza said, smiling brightly.

"Ye-e-e-e-sssss," agreed Sam and Chris.

Chris has a huge crush on Bruce Johnson and she'll do almost anything to keep him away from Jannette Sansibar. Then a dolphin in need enters the scene, changing Chris's whole life . . . and Bruce's, too!

Watch for SITTING PRETTY #4 *A Chance for Chris*

SUZANNE WEYN

Suzanne Weyn is the author of many books for children and young adults. Among them are: *The Makeover Club*, *Makeover Summer*, and the series NO WAY BALLET. Suzanne began baby-sitting at the age of thirteen. Later, while attending Harpur College, she worked as a waitress in a hotel restaurant. Suzanne grew up on Long Island, N.Y., and loves the beach. Sailing, snorkeling, water-skiing and swimming are some of her favorite activities. In SITTING PRETTY she is able to draw on these experiences.

Suzanne now has a baby of her own named Diana, who has two terrific baby sitters—Chris and Joy-Ann.